THE SIREN AND THE SWORD

MAGIC UNIVERSITY

Cecilia Tan

ra(/)enous
romance ™

ℛℛ
RED SILK
EDITIONS

First published in paperback in 2010 by
Red Silk Editions
500 Third Street, Suite 230
San Francisco, CA 94107

First published as an e-book in 2009 by
Ravenous Romance
100 Cummings Center
Suite 123A
Beverly, MA 01915
www.ravenousromance.com

ISBN: 978-1-59003-208-4

Cover design by April Martinez
Printed in Canada

TCP

10 9 8 7 6 5 4 3 2 1

The paper used in this publication meets the minimum re-
quirements of the American National Standard for Information
Sciences—Permanence of Paper for Printed Library Materials
Z39.48-1992 (R1997).

This book is a work of fiction, and any resemblance to persons
living or dead is purely coincidental.

Dedication

THIS BOOK is for all the grown-ups out there who believe in magic.

Acknowledgements

THANKS TO the passel of my fellow writers and readers who helped out with suggestions, proofreading, and shuttling me interesting historical tidbits on poetry, Harvardiana, and so on: Frances Selkirk, Lauren P. Burka, Catt Kinsgrave, Jordan, Claudia, Amy, and Lisa. To my super staff at Circlet Press, especially Jennifer, Jennifer, and Jennifer, who helped keep me sane through the writing of the book (or maybe you helped keep me crazy). And to corwin for always being there.

Prologue

THE ELWYN Library had a special kind of quiet: not silence at all, but a strange mix of the echoes of nothing in the high stone spaces in the reading room and the stifling hush of the mass of paper that was its collection. During the day, the sound of a footfall or of a page turning would be swallowed up. At night, the hush was hypnotic, like the steady sound of rainfall or wind rushing through the trees.

The student's head began to nod. He jerked awake, once, twice—but there was nothing around to keep him awake. He was alone in the library after hours, all the lights doused except for the reading light he'd brought with him to illuminate his cubby. He'd stayed hidden until after the building had closed, eager to spend the entire night with the precious texts he needed for his term paper.

But in the darkest hours of the night, he was beginning to feel the pull of sleep, of dreams. His head sank once again toward the page.

He jerked upward again. *Was* that a noise? Had he heard something after all?

He turned off the light. Could it be a security guard? Or another student with the same idea as him? He crept away from his desk deep in the stacks, past shelf after shelf of ancient texts, tiptoeing as he went.

There, a soft sound—like a sigh! He froze. Just on the other side of the bookshelf he was standing beside.

He felt her before he saw her, a warm hand reaching around his middle, startling him at first. But he could smell her perfume, feel the softness of her lips across the back of his neck. "Sarah?" he whispered. It must be her; his girlfriend was the only one who knew where he had gone tonight, and she must have planned this little surprise.

"Shhhhhh," came the reply, and it turned him on that she was being so secretive. Her hands opened his fly and pushed down his pants. He could feel her fingernails scratching lightly at his balls and he leaned his arms against the shelf in front of him while her fingers wrapped around his lengthening erection.

He moaned as she stroked him, then gasped as she raked the nails of her other hand under his shirt down his back, and dropped to her knees. Her wet mouth replaced her hand on his cock and he bit his lip, trying to keep quiet. Sarah had never been like this, so forward, so eager. They still hadn't had intercourse yet, just heavy petting, and she had only gone down on him once, but—

Maybe she was just waiting for the right opportunity? he wondered, as her tongue was doing wicked things to his cock. It had been frustrating, taking it so slowly, but rewarding at the same time, learning each other's bodies and how to touch and pleasure each other.

She must have read up on blow jobs or something, though, as she seemed to have perfected some truly expert techniques—if how close he was to coming was any indication.

Just when he was nearly there, though, she pulled back. "Sarah?" he tried to ask again, looking down in the dark, but he could not make out her face in the shadows. The library building had almost no windows in the stacks and very little ambient light seeped in from outside. Quite suddenly she leaped up, wrapping her arms around his neck, and her legs around his waist, and he gasped as he felt the velvet wetness engulfing his prick that had to mean she had impaled herself on him. *I thought we were going to wait!* he thought, but he wasn't about to try to interrupt her when she was so very determined. His arms went around her reflexively, then slid down to her buttocks to support her weight.

She felt like she hardly weighed anything as she rocked against him, milking his cock with her body and grinding herself against him while digging her nails into his shoulders. He helped her to move as best he could, as she seemed to bring herself off, much to his amazement, then keep going. *I'm not wearing a condom!* he thought suddenly, but she was the type who would have planned everything out. If she had waited in here, sneaked in to surprise him like this, then surely she had taken precautions.

He had no choice anyway. She was wringing his orgasm out of him before he knew it, clinging hard to him until his softening cock slipped wetly from her. Then she sprang back, leaving his arms suddenly empty and cold. "Sarah?" He took a step forward.

And jerked awake, lying with his face in a book.

Man, what an intense erotic dream. Maybe he was more frustrated about Sarah than he'd thought? He went back to studying, hoping he hadn't drooled in the book he was using.

It wasn't until he went to the restroom an hour or so later that he realized his pubic hair was a bit matted. Had it been a wet dream? But his underwear was dry.

And it wasn't until the next night when he got undressed in front of his roommate, and his roommate commented on the pattern of fingernail marks on his shoulders, that he believed it hadn't been a dream.

September

KYLE LOOKED at the map in his hand, then at the red brick buildings in front of him, standing like sentinels all around a grassy courtyard crisscrossed with pedestrian paths. The map was artfully done in cheery colors, with helpful tips and descriptions in word bubbles, as if each building were a cartoon character describing itself to the visitor. But the buildings he was looking at didn't match the map. For one thing, there were too many of them.

Maybe every building isn't actually shown on the map? he wondered. *Or maybe I'm in the wrong quadrangle? Or maybe this is all a test to see if you're REALLY smart enough to be allowed in to Harvard.*

He quashed that thought quickly. Kyle Wadsworth hadn't exactly always led a privileged or easy life, but the scholarship he was slated to receive proved he was good enough for Harvard. Well, at least, they'd said he was slated. The interview was just a formality, they said. The scholarship was as good as his, and with it, a new life could begin. He shifted his tie nervously. Now if only he could arrive on time, he might be getting somewhere. He'd been looking forward to this weekend desperately. Once the interview was out of the way, he would have the whole weekend to explore the city and the campus and—

and whatever. Kyle didn't even know what exactly he wanted to do, only that his blood had sung when he'd realized it meant a chance to get away from the house, away from Great-Aunt Agatha, away from the life he couldn't wait to leave behind.

He was already eighteen, a high school senior, and desperately ready to start his adult life. Or, at least, college student life.

But adults and students alike were supposed to be able to read maps.

Perhaps the map was just an artist's rendition and not to scale. He checked the printed e-mail he had folded in his jacket pocket. *Enter through the gate and then third building on your right*, it said.

One, two, three. This building looked a little older than the one next to it, its archway made of solid stone and the double doors of heavy wood. But when he pulled on the brass handle, it swung inward easily.

Kyle found himself in a carpeted hallway, which was a good sign. Jove had told him once that at universities the administrative buildings had carpets, and classroom buildings didn't, so he must be on the right track. At the very least, there was bound to be a secretary somewhere in here who could tell him if he was in the right place. The first door on the left was open, and he was about to step through it when a raised voice stopped him.

"Miss Torralva! You know perfectly well I do not believe these vile rumors, which are clearly nothing more than an attempt to undermine our authority and create hysteria."

It was a man's voice, speaking in clipped tones. He didn't have an accent, but the way he spoke reminded Kyle of British actors on TV.

A woman answered him. "Come now, Quilian, there's no need to be so harsh on the girl."

"Mistress Finch, I would appreciate if you would stay out of these matters..."

"And I would appreciate if you would not shout at my students."

Then a younger woman's voice. "I'm sorry to have disturbed you, Dean Bell. Never mind, Ms. Finch. It was a waste of time to come here."

"See that you don't do it again," the man said, and strode forcefully from the room, colliding with Kyle outside the door. Kyle found himself on his ass, looking up at a blond man in graduation robes, then scrambling out of the way as if the man were about to kick him.

Instead the man frowned and demanded, "Who are you?"

"Er, Kyle Wadsworth," he said, climbing to his feet and straightening his jacket. "I'm here for an admission interview?"

The two women he had heard were now standing in the doorway, too, looking at him curiously. "Interview?" said the older of the two, who looked to be perhaps forty. *She's a librarian*, Kyle thought, taking in a quick impression of her hair in a bun and glasses perched on her nose.

The librarian called behind her, "Helena, was there a prospective student scheduled to come in today?"

Kyle looked back and forth between the imposing, angry man and the younger woman in the door, who was presumably a student. She had wavy black hair, pinned back with barrettes, and eyes such a dark brown, they were almost black. No, maybe they *were* black, but her expression was warm. She was looking at him with a mix of sympathy and curiosity, stifling a smile.

"Um, hi," Kyle said in her direction, then turned back to the man still staring at him. "I'm the Pollock Scholarship recipient?" he ventured, hoping this might ring a bell. "I'm sure the e-mail said my interview was today, two o'clock..."

"You're in the wrong building," the man said, and pointed at the wall in the direction of the next building over.

"But Dean Bell," the girl piped up, "how could he even find...?"

"Silence." Bell's glare was as sharp as his voice. "Mr. Wadsworth, was it?" When Kyle nodded he went on slowly, as if Kyle might be too stupid to understand if he spoke any faster. "You. Do not. Belong. Here."

"Um, okay, sorry, I was just following the directions, third building and all," Kyle stammered. "I guess I wasn't supposed to count the one on the corner? Or maybe I was supposed to..."

"Mr. Wadsworth." It was the librarian again, and she and Dean Bell glared daggers at each other for a moment. "Before you move on, would you sign our visitor register? Our department doesn't get very many, you see, and our funding for tea and cookies will be cut if we can't prove a certain amount of interest. Right through here." She stepped aside and indicated the open doorway.

"Oh, sure. Anything to help...?" He dared a smile at the girl, who was watching him with that same open curiosity and a hint of a smile. She was wearing brown corduroy jeans with a flower embroidered on the pocket and he wasn't sure why he noticed little details like that, but he tucked it away in his head for later. Maybe he'd get a chance to run into her again.

Inside the office was a large, wooden reception desk which, like much of Harvard, looked like it was either from pre-1800 or like it was *made* to look that old. Behind the desk sat a pretty blond woman whose lipstick was rather bright. She set a large, leather-bound book on the desk, facing Kyle. The leather creaked as she opened it and she pointed to a cup of pens next to it.

They were all watching quite closely while Kyle took a step forward. Maybe this was the psychology department and this was all some kind of experiment on him? He reached into the pens and pulled one out, hissing sharply as he felt something prick his finger. *Great. Now I've cut myself and I'll be bleeding all through the interview. Way to make an impression.* He decided he had best just sign his name and get out of there as soon as possible. Maybe he could hurry next door and stop the bleeding in the men's room or something.

He touched the pen to the first empty line in the ledger and felt a curious shock go through his arm. *This has got to be some kind of weird experiment! Or maybe a reality TV show.* But he signed his name in flowing letters, hoping the reddish tinge to the ink didn't mean he'd bled onto the page, or at least hoping they didn't notice.

As he lifted the pen, he heard a bell tolling. Was he late? He whirled around to find they were all staring at him still. "Um, I...um...better be going..."

That bell just kept ringing though, so loud it was as if it were right in this building. What was going on? None of them moved until the bell ceased to ring, the women sighing in relief and Dean Bell crossing his arms over his chest.

"Well, thank you very much, Kyle Wadsworth," the librarian said. "I'm Madeleine Finch." She held out her hand to be shaken, and Kyle reluctantly set down the pen, but he didn't seem to get any blood on her hand as he shook it. "Welcome to Veritas. It would appear there's been a bit of a mix-up in your matriculation papers, though?"

Kyle stared at her. "Wait a second. That's it? I'm in? I only just sent the application. I thought I wouldn't hear until March..."

Dean Bell made a disgusted noise. "He's *your* stray puppy to deal with now, Mistress Finch. If anyone needs me, I shall be in my office." His tone of voice made it clear that anyone who needed him had best take a leap into the Charles River. He stalked out, robes fluttering behind him.

The receptionist immediately began digging in a file cabinet behind her, while the other two women kept looking at him with growing curiosity.

Kyle tried again. "Look, I'm supposed to have this interview today. I guess maybe I'm already pre-approved because I had to apply early in order to qualify for the scholarship, except I'm supposed to have this interview to, um, make sure I'm not an idiot in person, I guess, because Harvard doesn't admit idiots, or at least, that's the theory...uh..." He trailed off, realizing just how much like an idiot he sounded. The student hid her smile behind her hand.

"Mr. Wadsworth, may I ask you a personal question?" Mistress Finch folded her hands in front of her.

"Um, sure, please."

"Are you, by any chance, an orphan?"

He blinked. "Yes, I am, actually."

"But is Wadsworth your family name?"

How did she know these things? "Yes, yes, it is."

She paused. "Helena, did you find anything?"

The receptionist sighed. "Nothing, Ms. Finch."

Okay, and why do the women call her Ms. Finch, but the dean calls her Mistress Finch? He knew university society was supposedly different from everywhere else, but he'd never heard of that. Which one should he use? "Um, find what?"

"A record of your birth," Ms. Finch answered. "Well, you are a mystery but hardly the first one, Mr. Wadsworth. I'll just spell it out for you and see if it makes sense to you. The building you're standing in right now is not a part of Harvard. Well, it is, but it isn't. There's a secret university inside Harvard, known as Veritas."

Kyle blinked. "But isn't that what's on the signs outside? Harvard's motto..."

"The two institutions have an intertwined history," she went on. "Harvard is for the elite scholars, the future leaders of the world. Veritas is for, well, those with more arcane talents."

"Arcane?"

"Magical."

"Magical?" Kyle could still hear the bell ringing in his head. "You mean like wizards?"

The student snorted behind her hand. "We prefer the term 'magic users.' 'Wizards' is so patriarchal and un-PC."

Kyle shook his head, but although everything was as weird as some dream, it still seemed to be real. "So, sorry to be skeptical, but...you're saying I'm magical?"

"You wouldn't have even been able to see this building if you weren't at least a little Sighted," Ms. Finch said, "and you certainly wouldn't have been able to sign the matriculation register if you didn't have the power in your blood."

He checked his finger reflexively, but the bleeding had stopped and he couldn't even see where the pen had pricked him. "Um, the Dean didn't seem as convinced..."

"Yes, well, that was another test. He has the power of Voice. If you'd been a non-magical person, you'd have just turned and walked out as soon as he told you to." Ms. Finch sighed. "We're already two weeks into the semester, you haven't registered for any classes, and we need to find you a place to live."

Kyle looked back and forth between them. "You mean, start now? I, um, I'm supposed to, um..." Supposed to go back to a house where they didn't want him, a school where he didn't fit in, and count the days until he could leave. Maybe this was just the chance he had been waiting for. Hadn't he felt like this weekend was going to be the first step into a new life? Maybe it was just a bigger step than he'd thought. His skepticism shredded in the face of what felt like a real chance to change his life in a drastic way. "I mean, I'd love to start now."

"You had better. If you were completely unaware of the magical world until now, you have a lot of catching up to do. Helena, could you call up Admissions and see if you can get his file? It's hardly the first time we've had a mix-up between our office and theirs. Mr. Wadsworth, please make an appointment to see me, let's see, tomorrow at four o'clock. My office is on the second floor here in Peyntree Hall, and we can figure out your schedule then, after I check with the professors on what kind of openings we have." She paused and tapped her finger against her lips while she thought.

"I can take him over to Camella House," the student offered then. "We've got that foldout couch in our suite. And actually, come to think of it, Alex doesn't have a roommate and he's in a double..."

Ms. Finch debated for a moment. "Just for a few days, that sounds fine. He can draw cards later. Yes, Miss Torralva, I'd appreciate it if you could give Mr. Wadsworth here a bit of orientation."

"No problem, Ms. Finch." She stuck out her hand to shake Kyle's as Ms. Finch left the room. "I'm Jess Torralva. I'm a sophomore. You hungry? We could grab some pizza out in the Square, or do you have a suitcase somewhere that we ought to move up to the dorm?"

"Oh, um, yeah, it's at the bed and breakfast I stayed in last night." He followed her out the heavy doors and back down the stone steps. "So...'magic users' eat pizza?"

"Oh yeah. With newt's eyes and toadstools, though," she said, completely deadpan for a moment. Then she burst out laughing. "My God, the look on your face!"

He grinned. "Anchovy and mushroom okay? Yeah? Okay, I'll buy." This day was getting better and better. First he thought he was going to go to Harvard. Then he found out he was some-how magical. And now he was going to have lunch with a pret-ty girl who seemed really nice and down to earth and didn't treat him like he was some kind of pond scum. Yes, a whole new world seemed to be opening up before his eyes.

* * * *

They made their way back to the suite where Jess lived in Camella House, another red brick building not that differ-ent from the others all around Harvard, Kyle noticed, though perhaps a bit smaller than some. It was three stories tall, with about fifty students in residence. The suite was a central room on the third floor with two beat-up couches, a coffee table, and a large TV screen. There were doors to what Kyle took to be several bedrooms. Just down the hall was a very small kitchen. Students had decorated their doors in various ways; some had notepads or white boards for people to leave messages, and it all looked, well, completely *normal*.

He and Jess had bought two pizzas and brought them back to the suite to eat. As they walked in, a shaggy-headed student was just closing his door. "Ho, Jess, is that for sharing?"

"Yes, Alex, it is," she said as she put the boxes down on the coffee table.

"Did you hear the bell ringing? Any clue what that's about?" Alex said as he eagerly tossed himself into an armchair, whatever errand he had been on forgotten. Kyle quietly remembered the bell that tolled when he signed the ledger. "I've never heard it ring so many times in a row," Alex added.

Jess didn't say anything about the bell right away. "Alex, this is Kyle. As of today, I guess, he's a freshman." She sat down on the couch and opened the box on top. Steam rose from the pizza and Kyle's stomach growled as he sat down next to her.

"Yeah, hi, Kyle Wadsworth," he said, holding out his hand for Alex to shake, and they both reached for a slice. "Um..."

Jess grinned. "He thought he was going to Harvard."

Alex's eyes went up at that. "A foundling? When did they figure out you belonged here?"

Kyle stopped with the slice partway to his mouth. "Um, just today. I walked into the Veritas admissions office by mistake."

Alex looked back at Jess. "The bell was ringing for him?"

Jess just nodded, nibbling carefully at the tip of her slice of pizza.

"The bell rang like...fourteen times."

"Is that bad?" Kyle asked, unable to contain his anxiety any longer. "I signed my name in this book and..."

Alex waved him off. "No, it's not bad. Just...unusual. When it rings, it means you've been accepted. It only rang twice for me. Although for Jess here, I think it rang six or seven?"

Jess shrugged, as if it was of no consequence.

Kyle forced himself to take a bite before getting sucked deeper into the conversation. "What's a foundling?"

Alex drew a long string of cheese from his slice with his mouth as two more students came in and Jess waved them over. When he'd snapped it off and devoured it, he went on. "Foundlings are usually magical children who get raised by non-magical families, oftentimes ones who have no clue about the kid. It's pretty common, actually. History's full of them. It's a problem, because fertility among magic users isn't great to begin with..." He shrugged. "I guessed foundling and not prodigy because of your name. There were some magical Wadsworths a couple generations back."

Kyle had managed to wolf down the rest of the piece while Alex was talking. "Prodigy?"

Alex investigated the second box and grunted with approval at finding the black olives. "Prodigy. Like Lindy here."

A girl with chestnut brown hair, suddenly sitting cross-legged at the end of the table and had a bite of pizza in her mouth so she couldn't answer, waved with her free hand.

"Lindy's from a non-magical family, and far as anyone knows she's the natural daughter of her mother and father, but she's got the Sight, among other talents." Alex turned to Jess. "Did you get anything to drink?"

"There's soda in the fridge," Jess said, nudging him in the direction of the small refrigerator in one corner of the room. "Anyway, Kyle, it doesn't matter how you got your magic. Just what you do with it."

Kyle got the feeling Jess was arguing a point she'd had to make many times before, and he wondered if she was a prodigy, too, and if there was some kind of stigma attached to that.

Lindy wiped her hands on her jeans. "Nice to meet you, I'm Lindy Carmichael. And this is Jeanie," she said, indicating the Asian-looking girl standing behind her. "And that's Randall, going into his room there."

A heavyset student in a polo shirt waved over his shoulder as he went into his room and put his books down. When he emerged, Kyle was surprised to see he was black, but with his hair bleached completely blond. "Hello. Randall." His hand was large and warm as he shook Kyle's. "And no, it's not my natural color. You can blame Alex for this."

Alex chuckled. "Yeah, horrible spellcasting accident."

"Really?" Kyle's eyes widened.

Randall snorted and took a seat, and a slice of pizza. "No. But let us just say that hydrogen peroxide and ethanol do not mix."

"That's Randall's way of saying don't get drunk if you have a bottle of hair bleach," Alex said with a sly shrug. "It *seemed* like a good idea at the time..."

"You could dye it back, you know," Jess pointed out.

Randall answered with a shrug of his own. "Why pretend it didn't happen? It will grow out, anyway. We're here to learn, right? Let's call it a learning experience and move on."

Kyle couldn't quite place Randall's accent. Something Caribbean, he guessed, but he wasn't sure. It wasn't like Rastafarian, and he didn't really have much experience with people from that part of the world.

They ate for a while after that, the various suitemates catching up with each other, but eventually the topic came back around to Kyle and the bell.

"So, wait," Lindy said. "You had no idea at all? Just walked in?"

"And got trampled by Dean Bell," Jess added. "Fortunately Madeleine was there to rescue him."

"Mwahaha," Alex laughed maniacally. "And a good thing, too, or Master Bell might have made a snack out of you."

Kyle laughed too, but blinking in confusion, still not sure where the jokes ended and real things started.

"Pffft. Dean Bell's bark is worse than his bite," Jeanie said, prompting more laughs from the others.

"So what house is he going to be in?" Randall asked.

"Ours, obviously," Alex said, now drinking from an open can of cola, his bare feet up on his chair.

"Well, temporarily," Jess said. "I told Madeleine he could crash here until she figures out where he's going. She said he would have to pull cards later."

"Cards?" Kyle said, feeling like most of what he'd said in the past hour had been one-word questions.

"Cards! There's an idea." Alex climbed out of his chair, going directly over the arm toward the door to his room, and then coming back with a pack of cards. "Has anyone ever done a Tarot reading for you?"

"An old lady read my palm once, on the boardwalk in Santa Cruz..."

Alex waved him quiet. "No, no. I mean with Tarot cards."

Jess moved the pizza boxes aside and Alex spread his deck out on the low table, face up. Kyle peered at the pictures, which were more colorful and varied than typical playing cards, and yet still resembled them somewhat. Alex gathered them back up and shuffled the deck.

The others all watched, a sense of anticipation filling the room. "This isn't going to hurt or anything, is it?" Kyle asked.

"The truth always hurts," Jeanie quipped, and they all laughed, but it wasn't a cruel laugh.

Alex held out the deck. "Cut the cards, then pull one out."

"Okay." Kyle took the pack, cut it in the middle and set it down on the table, pulling the top card and looking at it. "Am I supposed to show it to you?"

Alex grinned. "Yes, you're supposed to show it to me. What do you think this is, a magic trick? Oh, duh." More laughter. "Go on."

Kyle slapped it down on the table like a blackjack dealer and Jess and Lindy gasped.

"The Ace of Swords," Alex said solemnly. Kyle waited for him to break into a grin, but his face remained serious.

Kyle finally turned to Jess. "What's that mean?"

Lindy made a scornful noise. "It doesn't mean anything. Alex isn't a soothsayer and probably neither are you. But the swords are the suit of Gladius House. Here in Camella, we're the cups. The Ace *does* usually refer to someone on the start of a journey..."

Jeanie snorted. "No wonder you only got a B on that exam. The Ace of Swords, without any other context, usually means The Hero. Think Prince Charming with his sword drawn, going off to slay a dragon."

Randall made a skeptical noise. "It can also signify the beginning of a great intellectual journey, though. The blade is Occam's Razor, and the light you see shining in the card is the light of reason."

Alex rubbed his hands together gleefully. "Draw two more cards, Kyle. Let's have one that's past and one that's future."

Kyle nodded, but hesitated with his hand over the deck. "Should I cut again? Or shuffle again?"

"You should do whatever you feel is right," Jess said seriously.

Her dark, dark eyes seemed to be telling him everything would be all right if he just went with the flow. Kyle let out a breath. "Okay."

He turned up two more cards. An appreciative murmur went around the table. "Your past, three of pentacles. Your future, three of cups."

"Cups, that's you guys, right?" The card showed three young women, dancing and drinking, looking very happy and festive.

Alex grinned. "Could be. The three of cups tends to mean good luck. Everything's going to work out. There'll be abundance and plenty."

"Three is the magic number?" Kyle tried.

Alex nodded. "You catch on quick. The three of coins here means hard work. You worked hard to get here."

Randall pointed to the cards. "It's usually meant as a pinnacle of craft, though. Given that you don't know anything at all about magic, yes, I guess Alex is right. You worked hard to get to Harvard, I guess."

Alex tapped the deck of cards. "And now for a prediction on what will happen to you...tonight." Kyle could practically hear a drum roll in the background. Alex tapped the deck again. "Go on, pull one more, Kyle."

Kyle put his hand on the top card, then turned it over slowly. The card showed two people, naked, in a close embrace. A very close embrace.

"The Lovers," Alex said, solemn again, then gave a sly look to Jess. "Perhaps you won't be sleeping on the couch after all...?"

Jess was blushing a deep red, but wasn't making any protestations. Kyle's eyes were probably as big as saucers. "Um, I, Jess..."

Jeanie got to her feet and made a disgusted sound. "Really, Alex, sleight of hand? Why don't you show him the other card you have up your sleeve?"

Kyle looked back and forth between them. "That was a trick?"

Jeanie wrinkled her nose. "He's also got the Three of Swords. Go on, show him."

Alex sheepishly pulled the card from his sleeve, handing it to Kyle. It showed a red heart, pierced through by three swords. "It means heartbreak, obviously," Alex said.

Jess got to her feet. "Come on, Kyle. Let me show you the library and some of the other campus buildings. We'll leave the card tricks to the jokers."

Kyle followed her, wondering what exactly had just happened.

* * * *

Jess was the perfect hostess for the next few hours: polite, friendly, but a little distant as she took him around the campus, showing him some facilities shared between the magical students and the normal ones, like the bookstore and the swimming pool; and the ones for magical students only, like Mormallor Hall, where the Alchemy labs were, and the Sassamon Ritual Arts building, which housed many magical artifacts, museum-style, and had a large underground chamber that reminded Kyle of a cathedral, except it was perfectly round and the colorful stained glass 'windows' were illuminated from behind by some light source that was not the sun.

As they made the rounds, Kyle learned a little more about Jess herself. She was a sophomore, and she hadn't declared her major yet, but she was thinking about Healing Arts, even though most people thought Esoteric Arts was more her style. He gathered that there were various departments, just like in a normal university, including Alchemy, Soothsaying, and Ritual Arts.

She also filled him in on the need for secrecy, and the history of Veritas, which went "underground" in 1692 because of the Salem Witch Trials. Technically, to the "real world," they were Harvard students, and if Kyle went on to a normal life as something like a banker or whatever, he'd be considered a Harvard alumnus. "But who would become a banker or something boring if they could do something magical?" Kyle had asked, which had made her laugh and admit that not many did.

They were having a look through the Elwyn Library collection of magical texts when Kyle lost her for a few moments. The labyrinthine shelves were packed with fascinating books with names like *Battle of Wills: When the Geas Becomes a Curse* and *Man is a Flightless Bird: Keys to Levitation*. At one point he turned to whisper to her, and found she was not behind him as he'd thought.

"Jess?"

He had the feeling someone was watching him, though. Was she playing hide and seek? He went further down the row, where the lights were not on. Each shelf had a timer switch at the end so that an absent-minded scholar could not leave the lights on in a given section of the stacks, nor could one pore over the books too long before being reminded to keep moving. Kyle did not bother to go back to the end of the shelf to turn the switch, instead pressing deeper into the shadows. "Jess?" he whispered again.

"—es," he thought he heard an answering whisper. Yes? Did she say yes?

He felt a hand brush over the back of his bare neck and goose bumps rose. He froze, then felt a soft finger trace the shape of his ear. "Jess?" he said a little louder.

The lights came on suddenly and there she was at the end of the row, her hands on her hips. "There you are. Didn't I tell you how these lights worked?"

"Oh, um, yeah." Kyle looked around him but there was no sign of whoever had been teasing him. It had to be her, but she had gotten to the end really quickly. He thought about how deeply she had blushed when Alex had slipped The Lovers onto the pile. He hurried to meet her. "Sorry about that. Um, hey, so... your friends are great and everything, but...but what do you say to having dinner together? I mean, just you and me."

Jess's black eyes seemed to deepen under the fluorescent lights as she looked up at him. "Are you sure?"

Kyle blinked. "Why wouldn't I be? Jess, you're a...a great girl. I really like you. It...it doesn't have to mean more than just dinner if you don't want it to."

She motioned him to follow her and as they were going down the stone stairs of the library, she answered. "I'd like that."

"For it to be just dinner?"

"For us to have dinner together. Without any expectations, I mean. It might be just dinner...it might not." Her face was angled toward the sunset, hidden by the buildings, the sky between the dark shapes of the trees in the courtyard turning purple.

"That's what I mean," Kyle said. "You know, a date, but the find-out-whether-there-will-be-a-second-date kind of date, rather than the already-committed-to-giving-a-relationship-a-try kind of date."

That made her laugh. "Okay. I can go along with that."

"Good. Just, um, not too expensive a place. I'm kind of on a budget..." He grinned at her sheepishly.

"All right." She linked her arm with his. "I really don't care where we go. In fact, let's go somewhere we don't have to put on nicer clothes. You like Mexican?"

"Mexican is good. Or what about Spanish? I walked past a Spanish place on the way to campus this morning?"

She made a face, then looked at him curiously. "I'm really picky about Spanish food," she said.

"Oh, is that place no good?"

She stopped walking and faced him. "You really don't know anything about the magical world, do you?"

He shook his head, wondering what Earth-shattering thing she was about to tell him. "Is it a *faux pas* to eat Spanish food because of...of the Inquisition or something?"

She burst out laughing. "No, no." Her face was alight with mirth and he wondered what else he could say to make her laugh like that. Only, intentionally. "You don't know much about the Inquisition, either, I'm guessing."

"Um, beyond that it happened and that Monty Python made fun of it, not really," he admitted. "I'm supposed to be taking European history this year—except it looks like I'm not going to, since I'll be here."

She smiled. "You're cute. Okay, sure. Let's have Spanish food. I'll order. Come on."

She took him by the hand, which for some reason made Kyle's heart do happy flips in his chest, and led him toward the nearest gate into Harvard Square.

* * * *

Jess apparently did know a lot about Spanish food. Not only that, but she spoke Spanish, which led to Kyle wondering if Torralva was a Spanish name, which led to Jess finally telling him it was a very old magical family name.

"He was basically one of the most famous enchanters in Spain in the early 1500s," she said. "He was the healer to Charles V, and reputed among his enemies to be a necromancer, while his supporters thought he talked to angels. The Inquisitors tried him for sorcery, imprisoned and tortured him for three years, and eventually they let him go to Rome..." She shrugged. "There are as many myths about him as there are truths. Let's just say that it would be a bit like you saying you were descended directly from Merlin."

Kyle was pushing his spoon through a kind of runny vanilla custard by then, trying to decide if it would be rude to lick the dish. "Are there descendants of Merlin?"

Jess shrugged. "If there are, they aren't saying so, anyway. England's had a really fucked-up history in terms of magical suppression, too, and they had some kind of internal civil war in the 1990s that came and went so fast that the other countries never even got to pick sides, from what I understand. But... yeah. People get all in a twist about my ancestry. It's a pain."

"Huh. I'm supposedly related to Henry Wadsworth Longfellow, but...well, now, come to think of it, Dean Bell did kind of raise an eyebrow at my name." He gave in and picked up the little glass dish and licked at the cream.

She nodded, seemingly unperturbed by his behavior. "Seems like many of the great American magical figures have been poets, too. Well, I suppose not just American. English language. Shakespeare, Blake..."

"Blake! William Blake?"

She grinned. "Yes, and William Shakespeare."

"Blake, who claimed to have breakfast with an angel every morning?"

"Yes, that Blake."

"Wait, so are angels real? You said your ancestor talked to them, too..."

She held up her hands. "Slow down, slow down. The first thing you're going to find when you explore the magical world is that a lot of what you know is true. The second thing you'll find, though, is that nothing is as you've been taught. Come on, let's walk while we talk."

She left money on the table, and as Kyle was digging out his wallet, she waved at him to put it away, as if annoyed he'd even try to pay any of it. Kyle wondered if that meant it wasn't as much of a date as he'd hoped after all, but he was still too fascinated by her and all she had to say to argue about it.

They walked back toward the subway station, where street musicians were playing. Across the way, in front of a bookstore, a man was juggling while riding a unicycle. "So the first thing you have to get used to, if you have pre-conceptions of magic, is that there's no such thing as good or evil," she said, as they walked along. The air was still warm and plenty of people were walking the streets at this hour. "There isn't 'black magic' and 'white magic' and although there's almost certainly a God, if there are angels or devils they don't actually have anything to do with what we do."

"But wouldn't it be evil to use magic to kill?" he asked.

She shook her head. "You can get into what the definition of evil is. Is killing evil? Are animals that hunt for their food evil? Are we, for eating meat?"

He thought about it for a moment. "But animals need to eat. It's different when one man kills another."

"Is it? What if they are at war, or it's self defense? What if one of them is suffering and the other one is releasing him from suffering?"

"Well, okay, but what if the only reason the one killed the other was...for power? Not to survive or defend his family or whatever, but just because it would further his ends?"

Jess turned to look at him as they walked. "Then is it the killing itself that's evil, or the motivation behind it? Desire for power could drive a man to do many things other than kill. Rape, pillage, embezzle, lie...is there something special about death?"

"Hm, I guess not." It had seemed so obvious a minute ago. "I guess that's why they say 'power corrupts'?"

"And 'absolute power corrupts absolutely,'" she quoted. "But when it comes to magic," and she said the word *magic* a little quieter than the others, "it is a power. So is physical strength, or intelligence. But fire, for example, is not good or evil. It has the power to destroy, to burn down a forest or a building, but we couldn't live without light or heat, could we? And we harness the power of fire to run machines, light our cities, build things, et cetera. Fire itself, though, is just a power—and magic is like that. A force of nature that can't really be judged by human morality."

He nodded. "So...what can I do with...with magic?" He followed her lead, saying the word most quietly at the end of his sentence.

"That remains to be seen, doesn't it? Just like you can have two equally intelligent people but one will be good at math and the other at language, we'll have to find out where your talents lie." She led him up past another group of street musicians. "Have you ever had prophetic dreams, or the sudden feeling like you knew what was about to happen?"

He thought about it. "Not really."

"If you can't think of an incident right away, you probably aren't prophetic," she said. "Usually, if you've had one of those dreams... you don't forget it. It stays with you, almost like it haunts you until it comes true."

Kyle walked a little faster so he could see her face as they made their way up the sidewalk. "Do you have that kind of dream?"

"I only did once," she said, pausing in front of the window of a natural foods store, then walking a bit more slowly down a side street. "I was thirteen. I dreamed I was at a masked ball, everyone was dressed for what must have been Carnavale in Venice. There was music and wine and dancing...then this man, dressed like some kind of prince or courtier in a black-and-white mask, took my hand and kissed it, and gestured to the dance floor..." She stopped again, this time looking into the window of an art gallery, except she wasn't seeing the glass sculptures or jewelry displayed there, Kyle thought. She was seeing the images of her dream.

She looked up at him suddenly and shook herself. "Um, yeah, so I dreamed I found my true love at Carnavale in Venice, and the next morning I woke up to find I had gotten my period for the first time." She was blushing.

"And have you ever been to Carnavale in Venice?" Kyle asked.

She shook her head. "I figure I'll go when I finish school. That doesn't mean the dream will come true, of course. It could mean a lot of things that I won't realize make sense until after they happen. I haven't had another one like that, so I don't think I'm prophetic, anyway. But we were talking about you." She started walking more quickly, and Kyle was amazed to find the street they were now walking down seemed to lead right back to the campus. He wondered if that was magic, or if his sense of direction was just wrong. "Do you have a green thumb?" she went on. "Or can you tell when someone's sick or hurt?"

He shook his head.

"Hmm. Well, Madeleine—that is, Ms. Finch to you, unless you end up in Camella House for real—will probably have some tests to help you determine your aptitudes, maybe to help you pick out classes. Although I'm betting she's going to put you right into History of Magic and some stuff like that."

Kyle made a face. "Sounds a bit dull."

"And probably a class in poetry."

"Poetry?"

"After all, you're descended from Longfellow, right?"

"Huh. My cousin used to say I had a way with words."

"Maybe you'll be the next great English-language poet and word mage." Now she looked up shyly. "They say no one's ever perfected a love potion that really works, after ten centuries of trying, but that a love poem can be irresistible."

Here her eyes looked like deep pools, like he'd never find what was at the bottom of their depths. He was hardly aware of having stopped walking, one hand catching hers as she faced him. "Let's go back to your room," he said.

Her smile was as knowing and alluring as the Mona Lisa's. "You're right. You know just what to say."

They didn't say anything as she led the way back to the dormitory, not holding Kyle's hand this time, yet he felt as close as if she had, as if an invisible line were connecting them.

Jess didn't speak again until she had closed the door behind them. Her room had two beds, from which Kyle supposed she had a roommate, but she latched the door behind them. He decided not to worry about it. There were other things grabbing his attention. Like her hand on his cheek. "Despite my name,

I'm not very experienced," she said, standing so close he could feel the front of her shirt brushing his.

"Name?" he asked, trying to remember where in the Torralva story there was anything about sex. Maybe he'd better study up.

"Never mind," she said. "I really like you, Kyle. I do. I just don't want you to be disappointed."

He slid his arms around the small of her back, which pulled their hips together to create a center of heat between them. "Whatever you want to do is fine. I'm not very experienced either." He held back from telling her that he'd in fact been considered a total loser in high school and that scoring a gorgeous, smart, funny, and kind girl like her would have been out of the question. There was being honest, and there was oversharing. "I mean, really." *You just met me. I, um, I wasn't even sure we were going to go beyond the good night kiss, it being a first date and all...*

He didn't voice those thoughts either. Did he really have the power to say the right thing? He let out a slow breath and tried to imagine he did.

"Just tell me when I should stop," he said, tilting her chin up so that he could kiss her.

"Okay," she whispered, just before his lips touched hers.

* * * *

Kyle woke up in an unfamiliar bed, his face pressed against a wall that had been painted so many times it felt almost rubber-coated. It took him a while to remember—oh, Jess's bed.

Looked like Alex's prediction had come true after all.

The sheets were twisted all around him like he was some kind of Greek statuary, and Jess was nowhere to be seen. The bed was so narrow he was amazed they had fit in it, except that they had literally slept in each other's arms.

He lay back, blinking against the sunlight coming in her window, wondering when her roommate was going to be back, and thinking about the night before.

She was so beautiful.

She had let him undress her, bit by bit, kissing newly bared skin, sometimes giggling, sometimes sighing, depending on whether the place uncovered was ticklish or not. Until yesterday, he would have described the whole experience as magical.

He dragged some clean clothes out of his bag and got out his toothbrush. On his return from the bathroom, he was unsurprised to find Alex lounging on the couch with a book balanced on his chest. Kyle waved to him.

"Good night, hey, Ace?" Alex said, sitting up to make room for Kyle to sit down if he wanted.

"Yeah, I guess so." Kyle grinned as he realized he was blushing. "Not...not what I would have expected."

Alex raised an eyebrow. "She give you the talk about ritual purity?"

"Um, yeah," Kyle said, wondering suddenly if Alex had dated Jess before, or if they were just close friends, or if all magical girls had this thing about how far they were willing to go? "I mean, we'd already said kind of, that we weren't going all the way. But, yeah." Jess had explained it wasn't so much morality that turned her virginity into a prize as much as the amount of power it had potentially for certain kinds of ritual magic. His, too, she'd explained. "I guess it makes sense." All those virgin sacrifices in stories, and virgins and unicorns, and...he hadn't needed it explained twice. There had been plenty they could do that was new to him, after all, and they'd both had a very, very good time, at least as far as Kyle could tell. She didn't seem the type to fake it. "I hadn't expected to hook up with someone so fast, though. I, uh, I don't really know if it was just for last night, or just until I find somewhere else to live, or what."

Alex chuckled. "That sounds like Jess. She'll tell you the meaning of the star you were born under instead of giving you directions to Star Market."

"She's...amazing." Kyle blushed again as he realized how lovestruck he sounded.

Fortunately, Alex just agreed. "Yeah. So what are your plans for today? You're meeting with Finch or something and then...?"

"I have no idea. I was supposed to fly back, but I guess that's not happening. Unless she changes her mind after all and kicks me out..." Kyle found Alex staring at him with a thoughtful expression on his face. "What?"

"You know you signed the student register in blood, right?"

Kyle remembered the pinprick. "Oh, um, I guess I did."

"That's a kind of promise. And it's not as easy as just kicking you out," Alex said, as he leaned back and crossed his legs again, a sly smile coming over his face. "Or Morgana knows they would have gotten rid of *me* ten times over."

"You? Why?"

"Because, as Ms. Finch has quaintly put it, my middle initial ought to be *T* for trouble. Dean Bell put it much less quaintly." He shrugged.

"So you're saying they can't expel you?"

"They would have to do more than just expel me. They'd have to essentially kick me out of the magical world entirely. The PTBs can get pretty fanatical about secrecy. So you'd be looking at putting me under a geas never to speak a word about magic ever again. More likely, they'd make me forget it completely."

Kyle stared wide-eyed. "Holy crap. Er, what are PTBs?"

"Powers That Be, my friend. Don't worry, no one around here can understand half of what I say anyway." He stretched and yawned. "So what time's your meeting? I know Jess showed you around yesterday, but...there's a lot more to see."

Kyle got the feeling that what Alex would show him would probably be highly different from the "official" tour. "Four, at Peyntree Hall." He glanced back toward Jess's room.

"Today's what, Friday? She's at class until at least two. I'll show you where we eat and stuff. Come on."

Kyle grabbed his jacket and followed Alex out of Camella House. "Okay, you have the Sight, right? So, let's see, Jess probably showed you already, that's Gladius House there. Scipionis is right behind them where you can't really see. And the Elwyn Library just past that..." He pointed in the direction they were walking. "Most of the houses at Harvard have their own dining halls, but Camella doesn't...I'm honestly not sure why. So we eat at the others'. Which would you prefer? The snobs or the bookworms?"

Kyle thought for a second. "Isn't there a fourth house?"

"Nummus. But it's a hike and I'm hungry. The menu's the same, only the company's different."

"Why would you want to eat with the snobs?"

Alex let another sly smile onto his face. "Because I'm a troublemaker."

"Oh. Then, how about the bookworms?"

Alex laughed. "You'll meet the snobs soon enough. If it really was you who rang the bell fourteen times, they're going to be crazy to meet you."

"Whatever," Kyle said. His stomach growled loudly. "Food is food."

They went past a large building built of gray stone with the shield and the word *Veritas* over the archway, then came to a very large, wooden-clapboarded house, sandwiched between the previous building and the next one, which looked rather more modern.

Alex led them up the steps to a brass doorknocker shaped like a lion. He rapped it twice and opened the door. Kyle glanced back at it as they entered, wondering what was special about the doorknocker, if anything.

But Alex did not explain. Just led him through a large sitting room lined with bookshelves except for right around the fireplace in one wall, and into an even larger dining room. Kyle guessed it would seat sixty or seventy students at once, though right now there were only maybe twenty seated and three or four milling around what looked like a large salad bar at one end. As they came deeper into the room, which was sunny from the tall windows all along one wall, Kyle could see there was a man in a white chef's hat and jacket at a serving area in a niche to one side. Presumably there was a whole kitchen behind him. Beyond the salad bar was a station just like the ones at fast-food places for filling your own drinks.

Alex picked up a tray from a cart and Kyle said, "So magic users drink soda?"

"And whatever else we can get our hands on. We're supplied by the same food service as the rest of the college." Alex led him to the large crocks of soup, hot entrees, and fresh-baked bread. Kyle read the labels on the crocks. *New England Clam Chowder* and *Vegetarian Tortilla Soup*. He ladled himself out some chowder, then followed Alex into the kitchen-y area.

The chef was behind a high divider so they could only see him from the shoulders up, but Alex seemed to have engaged the man in an animated conversation. "Yeah, so that's why I don't eat poultry," he was saying to the chef.

"Well, eat the pasta, then," the man answered, gesturing with a pair of tongs toward the serving counter. "There's a ham, peas, and asparagus topping for it, or red sauce. Or just butter, if your delicate constitution can't handle anything more."

"Ohh, you are cold. Is there grated cheese? Ah, I see it. I'm all set then." Alex gave the man a quick salute, then proceeded to serve himself ziti with red sauce and smother the entire plate in grated cheese. He popped the plate into a microwave oven.

Kyle finally saw the sign that listed the three lunch entrees and ended up getting a chicken cutlet from the chef, along with a little pasta and the ham and peas. Alex pulled the plate out carefully with two napkins as improvised potholders, and the two of them went to sit down in the main room next to a boy Alex introduced as Michael Candlin.

Michael had large round eyes and large round glasses to match. The food on his tray seemed to be entirely cold cuts and little cubes of cheese, and he was eating them one after the other with a fork. "Pleased to meet you. Wadsworth, was it? Any relation?"

"Um, yeah, sort of distant, but here I am." Kyle sat down and spooned up some soup. "My first day here, actually."

"Oh? A late arrival?"

Alex answered. "You could say that." He glanced at Kyle as if for permission to say more. Kyle just shrugged. "Kyle here didn't know until yesterday he was magical."

Michael's eyes got rounder and he seemed to hunch down in his seat. "That hasn't happened in a while."

"Not since I've been here, anyway," Alex replied. "Jess said the bell was ringing for him."

"Indeed? So, then, Kyle, what's your talent?"

Kyle had just slurped up some soup and found it nearly too hot to eat. He nearly dropped the spoon. "Oh, um, I don't know yet."

"Curious. Usually people show some weirdness by your age."

"Weirdness?"

"You know, speaking in tongues, or extraordinary luck or intuition, or understanding what animals say, or calling down lightning, or being struck by it but not killed..."

"No, no, nothing like that." Kyle shrugged. "As far as I can tell the only magical thing I've ever done was walk into the admission office in Peyntree Hall, sign the book, and apparently make the bell ring."

"Interesting," Michael said, and watched Kyle eat for a bit, as if Kyle were a fascinatingly interesting animal.

"We figure ol' Finch will probably have some test for him or something. Or maybe we just have to wait and see how he does." Alex was eating his pasta with such enthusiasm that Kyle was glad none of them was wearing a white shirt.

Kyle returned his attention to his food for a few minutes, then looked up when someone else approached the table. Two girls sat across from them and started chattering to Alex immediately. Before he could get the girls' names, another student came up to them, a pale-skinned boy with black hair. Kyle just stared as the newcomer slid his hands over Michael's shoulders and Michael tilted his face upward for a quick kiss of greeting.

They made almost a matched pair, though Michael's cheeks were a little rosier and his hair like straight silk, while the other's curled in small black tendrils. "Who's your new friend?"

Michael kept looking up at his friend. *Boyfriend*, Kyle corrected in his mind. "His name is Kyle Wadsworth. Seems to be a bit of a late bloomer."

The newcomer extended a hand to Kyle, who shook it. "Frost. Timothy Frost." Had his hand felt cooler than Kyle expected? Or was it— "Frost, like..."

"Robert Frost, yes. Hmm, Wadsworth, eh?"

Michael shook his head and spoke as if he'd just read Frost's mind. "He hasn't been assigned a house yet. Or shown any aptitudes."

"That is curious," Frost said, moving away from Michael and taking the empty seat on the other side of Kyle. "No party tricks? No visions?"

Kyle opened his mouth to say "No, I..." then stared in disbelief as Frost snapped his fingers and a few fronds of some kind of plant appeared in the palm of his hand. He opened Kyle's limp hand and dropped them into his palm.

"You seem less than impressed?" Frost's eyes were ice blue.

"I, um, I've never seen anything like that before...?" Kyle stammered.

"Not a botanist either, I would guess," Frost said with a sniff. He snapped his fingers again and Kyle jumped as the long fuzzy flowers in his hand suddenly developed ice crystals.

"How did you do that?" Kyle said, too amazed to worry about the sneer Frost was giving him.

"He invoked his Name," Alex said, glaring daggers at Frost. "Yeah, I'd call that one a party trick, Frost."

Frost shrugged. "I'll always be able to prove who I am though, won't I? Put your eyes back in your head, Wadsworth. If they fall on the floor, they'll get dusty."

"How many times did the bell ring for you, Frost? Once?" Alex said, a toothy smile on his face.

Frost's pale cheeks reddened, but he didn't say anything in return. He just stood smoothly and returned to standing behind Michael's chair, running his hand over Michael's smooth dark hair possessively.

Michael looked up at him again. "Fourteen," he said.

"Are you sure?"

"According to Kimble, anyway."

Frost's eyes narrowed. "The cards will decide," he said with a shrug. "I'll see you later, darling." They exchanged another very quick kiss, then Frost left.

The two girls were glaring daggers at his back as he went and Kyle felt a bit better. "Honestly, Michael, I don't know what you see in him," one of them said.

Michael shrugged. "You wouldn't understand."

"Apparently not. But really, fourteen? Kyle, that's amazing." She had wavy red hair with blond highlights and reached across the table to shake his hand. "My name's Marigold, but I can't make marigolds come out of my ass," she said with a last glance toward the exit.

"I'm Kate," said the other. She had her straight brown hair pulled back in a pony tail. "Fourteen, hmm?"

"So they tell me," Kyle said. "I wasn't counting at the time."

"Isn't there something about fourteen?...Hmm." Kate got up quickly. "I think there is..."

Alex watched her hurry into the room with all the books, then disappear from sight. "Well, you just shot her afternoon, Kyle."

"What?"

"She's going to spend hours now trying to look up the reference she's trying to remember. Happens a lot here at Scipionis House."

"Ah." The bookworms, right. Kyle was still staring at the flowers in his hand, though the frost had melted to beads of water now. He set them down on his tray. "So that was...that was real magic? Or was it a sleight of hand?"

Alex shrugged. "Who knows for sure? A great magician never reveals his secrets."

Michael made a noise. "That's the first time I've ever heard you call him great."

"That was sarcasm, Mike," Alex said, rolling his eyes. "You really ought to dump him."

Michael pursed his lips. "I like him just fine. He's perfectly nice to me. Maybe if you didn't bait him all the time, he'd be nicer to you, too."

"Not too likely," said Marigold with a snort. "Oh, here comes Kate again, with Master Lester!"

Kyle turned to see the girl returning with someone rather professorial in tow. He was even wearing a tweed jacket with elbow patches, had a tuft of gray hair atop his head, and a pipe, though it was unlit. She was relating to him, from what Kyle could hear, the story of how Kyle had ended up at Veritas.

"Hmm, well, yes, you're right, there is a line about fourteen heralds in the prophecy, but well, hmm." The man walked up to Kyle, who got to his feet. "The prophecy," the professor said, "goes like this:

One will come from land and one will come from sea
And fourteen shall herald when first they lay eyes...

"You may have noticed though, Kate, that it doesn't say fourteen of what. Now the translation from the original Avestan to Magian dialect may be faulty, but it's largely assumed that the 'fourteen heralds' referred to here are fourteen angelic beings. Fourteen tolls of the bell, though, yes, it could be." The man coughed. "And you say your name is Kyle? How interesting then, that relates to another couplet in a few lines later:

The jasmine will meet the fairest flower of the field
And the narrows will be plied by the spirits beholden...

"Kyle, after all, being Scottish for 'narrows' or 'strait,' you see."

Kate beamed. "And what do you make of the fact that Frost just gave him a handful of flowers of the field, Master Lester?"

The man burst into hearty laughter. "Oh! As for that, my dear girl, well, I suppose you may count it if you want, but most interpretations of the 'flowers of the field' give it a much grislier meaning, usually referring to the stain of blood on the ground under each fallen soldier. But well, I suppose, a literal interpretation, how novel! Yes, must think about that. Thank you, my dear."

And with that, Master Lester turned and left the room.

"Kate's doing a semester project on prophecy interpretation," Marigold stage-whispered to Kyle. "It's kind of like literary criticism, only..."

"Only even more bullshitting," Alex finished.

Kate sat back down and stuck her tongue out at him. "At least I'm going to *do* my junior project."

Alex waved a hand. "Yeah, well, what's the rush? When I find the right topic, I'll go for it. I'm wasting everyone's time until I figure out what I want to do."

"Yeah, right." Kate got up with her cup in her hand and went to get a drink.

Marigold turned to Kyle and said earnestly, "You can basically take almost any of the old prophecies and, you know, between re-translation and metaphors and ambiguities, you can make it seem like they predict almost anything. Wars, assassinations, the weather..." She shrugged, but her eyes were quite serious. "That one Lester was quoting from, a series called the Avestan Prophecies, is about a kind of magical apocalypse, where we'd all disappear from the face of the Earth."

"Like the Rapture," Alex added.

"Rapture?" Kyle asked.

"You know, some Christians believe God is going to come down and judge everyone, then take those who are worthy off to Heaven? Right?" Alex said, looking around at the others for confirmation. "There was a church around here for a while putting up posters all over saying what the date and time was going to be, too. Then that day arrived and..."

"And?"

"Well, I don't think anything happened. You don't see those posters anymore, though."

Michael pushed his glasses up his nose. "Maybe that's because their God came and took them all away on that day."

Alex laughed. "I suppose I can't fault your logic there."

Marigold shook her head. "Anyway, the Avestan Prophecies, the first cycle in it is one of the oldest and most famous, so no wonder Kate was all over it. But it's also one of the least understood, worst translated, all that. Master Lester is one of the world authorities on it, though. They say he can recite the entire thing in like five languages."

Alex yawned. "Yeah, cool. Anyway, gotta go." He stood and Kyle followed. "See you all later."

They made their way back out into the sunshine of a perfect late September afternoon. "All right, let's see what else I can show you before you have to go to Finch's office."

Alex showed Kyle many interesting things that afternoon, but the memory that stayed with Kyle was of the stalks of timothy turning icy in his hand.

October

SONG

When we came home across the hill
No leaves were fallen from the trees;
The gentle fingers of the breeze
Had torn no quivering cobweb down.

The hedgerow bloomed with flowers still,
No withered petals lay beneath;
But the wild roses in your wreath
Were faded, and the leaves were brown.

T. S. Eliot, published in The Harvard Advocate when he was a student, around 1907

Kyle sat on the high stone bench outside Robinson Hall looking at the poem in his lap. Each time he read it, his mind seemed to go blank at the end. What was he supposed to say about this poem? *It's sad. Resigned. There's an inevitability about it.* That was about all he had come up with, and any half-wit could say those things.

There were probably all sorts of magical metaphors and meanings lurking within, of course, but he didn't know what they were. Was the wreath special in some way? Was that a reference to a pagan ritual, maybe? Or was it the sort of wreath put on a door rather than worn on the head? Well, no, "your" wreath...it definitely had to be the kind that was worn on the head.

Class was due to start in twenty minutes and he still didn't have anything prepared.

It didn't help that Frost was in this class, too. Frost seemed to know everything there was to know about poets and poetry. At least this one was a magical class. Kyle's other literature class, the one on actually writing poetry, was all mundane students, most of whom wrote truly awful poetry, too. At least in that class, he seemed to be doing well.

His other two classes were both magical: Introduction to Alchemy, and Soothsaying Practices in the English-Speaking World. He was barely keeping his head above water in them, but at least he had plenty of help. Jeanie Kwan was in the Soothsaying class and was happy to help him with it. She seemed to think the course was a gut, an easy A, and Kyle remembered how confident she had been that first night when Alex had done the Tarot reading for him. And Randall always had advice on Alchemy, as did just about everyone.

Life would have been easier, of course, if he'd just stayed at Camella House, where all his friends were. But fate hadn't dealt him that card.

It had dealt him the Ace of Swords.

He had gone to Madeleine Finch's office that Saturday as he'd been instructed. Her office had a much taller ceiling than he'd expected, and the windows were all set high near the ceiling, perhaps creating an optical illusion that the ceiling was higher than it actually was? She had set him without preamble into the green leather chair in front of her desk and handed him a pack of cards. "Best get this part over with," she said, as if she didn't have much enthusiasm for the process.

The backs of her cards had intricate designs and they were larger than regular playing cards. He shuffled them clumsily in his hands, then decided he'd best not go on with that too long or he might drop them all over the floor. He neatened the stack and turned up the top card.

A figure was painted there, white skin glowing as if in moonlight and black hair a bit wild, as if blown by the wind off the moor. Blue eyes stared past the sword he had upraised, directly at Kyle. "That looks a lot like Timothy Frost," he said.

Ms. Finch let out a huff of breath. "Indeed. And there's no question, the Ace of Swords means Gladius House for you. I'll let Dean Bell and Master Brandish know." She took a seat behind her desk and brought a computer screen to life. Its glow gave her glasses a bluish cast. Kyle blinked. He hadn't even noticed the computer before and it looked out of place now that he had. She tapped on the keys, then looked up at him. "You seem surprised to see we use e-mail."

"Oh, um, I guess so."

"Where we can, we've adopted the best system we can either for purposes of camouflage, or efficiency. We had magical means of instant communication long before the non-magical population did. But magic of any kind requires energy...well, so does e-mail, but it comes out of the plug on the wall and the university pays the bill. Trust me, e-mail is better than a magic mirror." She tapped on a few more keys and examined the screen.

"Now, I've spoken to a few people about fitting you into their classes, and honestly your choices may be a bit limited, both by your lack of prior knowledge and the fact that the semester is already three weeks old. I've also spoken to Admissions and it would appear you will be required to finish a year of English in order to receive your high school diploma, which they will require."

Kyle tried not to fidget as she looked at him. "Um, the others were saying it might be helpful if I told you what my aptitudes are."

"Indeed," she said. "And what are they?"

"Well, that's the problem. I seem to be a late bloomer."

"Ah. Yes, I suppose it would be too easy if you just waltzed in already an accomplished Seer or obvious prodigy in Enchantment." She tapped a few more keys and the sound of a printer coming to life whined in his ears. She stood and turned to get a page coming out of the printer behind her. "Here, have a look at this list. The simplest form of Soothsaying for us here is probably for you to pick out what looks most interesting for you, and let's hope you don't pick too many things that meet at the same time."

Thus he'd chosen his three magical classes, including Poetry: Analysis and Interpretation Through the Ages, and one regular English, in poetry writing. Ms. Finch thought maybe that was too much poetry, but it worked in the schedule and made Admissions happy, so she approved his schedule.

Kyle sighed and lay back on the bench in the shade of the building. It wasn't even properly a bench—it was more like the plinth of some long, low statue that had gotten up and walked away, and was high enough that he had to hoist himself up onto it. The doorway of the building was guarded by friezes of gryphons on either side, set into the walls. *Maybe there used to be a big one here,* Kyle thought. *Until it flew away.*

"Daydreaming again, Wadsworth?"

He closed his eyes with a sigh of resigned recognition, then dragged himself upright. "Hello, Frost." The figure approaching looked as pale as ever. *He's not a vampire. I've seen him in the sun,* Kyle thought, then made a mental note to ask someone whether vampires were real or not.

"I don't know what your layabout friend has told you, but it really won't do to wait until fifteen minutes before class to do your homework." Frost came to a stop a few feet away, his backpack held in one hand by a strap instead of slung over his shoulder. "Master Brandish really won't stand for slacking in Gladius House."

Kyle ran his hand through his hair, ignoring the dig at Alex. "I'm not slacking. I've been staring at this poem for...for days. But I just don't know what to say."

A tiny smile curled Frost's lip. "But I thought that was your knack, isn't it? For saying the right thing? Always knowing what to say?"

Kyle stared at him in shock. "Oh God, you're right. That's... that's usually true..."

Frost shook his head very slowly, as if saddened by this revelation and expressing deep sympathy and regret, except for the smirk. "Not much of an aptitude, if you ask me." He took two steps closer, coming almost all the way up to the plinth so he could lower his voice to say what came next. "Are you sure you're magical? What if you're one of those mundanes who just happens to be Sighted?"

"There are Sighted mundanes?" Kyle felt a cold trickle spiral down his spine.

"Of course. Most of them are harmless, or easily misdirected. But, hmm. You've seen an awful lot. Not sure you'd be allowed to keep your memories..."

"No!" Kyle jumped down, fists clenched. The book of poems fell with a thud. He could live without being magical, but he couldn't live without Jess. And he'd forget her if they put him under the Geas.

Frost waved a hand. "Don't be so dramatic. Pull your grades up and no one will even blink if you don't demonstrate an aptitude until you absolutely have to declare a major. You can buy yourself two years that way, you know. Now come on, it's nearly time for class."

Kyle stood there a moment longer as Frost drifted into the building. He shook himself and picked up the book. One minute he got the feeling Frost hated him and couldn't wait to see him given the boot; the next like it was just part of some game Frost played.

Just add Frost to the list of baffling things I don't understand in the magical world.

He went into the classroom. It was a small room with a large wooden table, and blue plastic chairs around it.

Professor Bengle was already there, writing some words on the board. Frost took the seat next to the head of the table, while Kyle took the one closest to the door, the furthest he could get from him. The others filed in as he opened the book to the poem and then his notebook, the page in front of him conspicuously blank. The professor turned to the group and took his seat. He had a graying mane of hair, which really did not fit the clothes he wore, Kyle thought. Today he was wearing a leather jacket and black jeans that looked like they belonged on someone in his twenties, not his...fifties? Kyle could only guess.

A few more students came in and took their seats. Kyle's stomach roiled. Each one of them had been given a different poem to interpret and present to the class last Thursday. He breathed a small sigh of relief as the professor did as predicted and started the presentations with Frost, then things would just go around the table. Each one them would give their interpretation and then the group would discuss the interpretation, picking it apart, some for, some against. That gave Kyle the space of five people's presentations to come up with something. He wasn't out of this game yet, wasn't on the path to expulsion and the Geas yet.

He stared at the words in front of him and they seemed to almost swim and hover above the page after a while. He wasn't listening to or absorbing any of the words being spoken at all. It was like being in a trance.

Quite suddenly, the student next to him, an Irish girl named Ciara, poked him in the ribs. "Your turn."

"Oh." Kyle looked up. Professor Bengle was smiling at him down the table with a benign and expectant look.

"Well," Kyle began. "This poem was written by Eliot while he was a student at Veritas, and it was never printed in his other books or anything, even his supposedly 'complete' poems. It was published in the literary magazine for Harvard, and he was an editor there, too." All of this, the other students in the class could have found in the notes in the back of the book, but a few of them were giving him, "oh, how interesting" looks, so he soldiered on.

He looked back at the poem. "Let me recite it." He cleared his throat and recited the lines, then found himself savoring the moments of silence at the end while the words sank into everyone's brains. His eyes locked with Frost's for a moment.

"This poem is about someone who is losing her magic," Kyle said suddenly.

Surprised looks around the table, and a bushy gray eyebrow raised in interest on Professor Bengle's face.

"We are constantly using the metaphor of the flower to represent magical power," Kyle went on. "Like with expressions like 'late bloomer.' The almost unspeakable sadness imbued in this poem is entwined with the helplessness of the poet or narrator. There's nothing he can do. It's only the very beginning of the waning, but he already foresees the disaster coming. I believe there's more to this poem, and that only the first two stanzas were put into the mundane magazine, but that probably somewhere in his papers, or maybe only in his head, there was more to this. Perhaps he only printed the first two stanzas because they easily lend themselves to mundane interpretation, and the following stanzas would have been too revealing. Or perhaps he excised them later, as this poignant moment of realization is the best expression of all that is to come."

The table burst into argument. "You can't mean that Eliot was referencing the Avestan Prophecy?"

"That's not the only prophecy that has that kind of thing in it, you know..."

"Magic loss is a common anxiety age after age, and surely Eliot could have drawn on this..."

And on and on. Kyle found he didn't have to say or defend anything. His eyes met Professor Bengle's down the table and he was gratified to see an approving nod before the professor argued a point with another student.

When class was over, Kyle wondered what Frost was going to have to say. But Frost just packed up his books and marched out quickly at the end, as if he didn't even see Kyle standing there by the door.

The professor, however, did. "Well, Kyle, that was a bold stroke today. Nicely done. Have you read much of Eliot's other poems?"

Kyle had to think. "Um, the Prufrock one, in English class last year. That was before I knew he was magical, though."

The professor nodded. "You might want to read *The Wasteland*, as well. Perhaps I'll assign it to you at the end of the semester for your final paper? Have a look at it anyway, and perhaps it'll resonate with you as this one did." He pulled on his leather jacket, then took a pair of dark sunglasses from the pocket. He slipped them on as the class exited the building and walked away without saying another word to Kyle.

Kyle wondered what the hell had just happened, exactly. But even if his sudden insight into the poem had seemed, well, sort of miraculous, he was afraid Frost was right. The ability to interpret a poem probably didn't stand up to being able to foretell the future. Or even conjure flowers.

* * * *

Kyle dragged himself up the stairs of Gladius House, wondering why his bag now seemed to weigh twice as much as usual. He hadn't slept very well the night before, but being sleepy and feeling like he could barely get his legs up the steps to the front door was something else entirely.

He pulled open the door into the vestibule, and it closed behind him as he was pulling open the inner door. The two doors created some kind of a vacuum and he couldn't get the inner door to open until the outer door had shut completely. *That's backwards*, he thought. It should be the other way around, right? He realized he didn't know enough about the science of air pressure and buildings to determine if it was that, or if some kind of magic was at work.

He finally pulled the door open enough to get through. The Gladius House doors opened directly into their common room, a high-ceilinged space with a fireplace on either side, tall windows, several bookshelves and chairs and couches scattered around. Above one of the fireplaces was a painting of a ship at sea, being tossed by a dark storm. Kyle had no idea if it was supposed to be a good painting, or if some alumnus of Gladius House had painted it and given a donation large enough for it to be hung.

He sat down by the fire, contemplating the climb up to his room. He was all the way up in what they called the "tower," though really it was just the cramped, rarely assigned room under the slant of the roof. The disadvantage of barely being able to stand up straight right at the center of the room was outweighed by the fact that he had the room to himself. *Just think, you could have been stuck rooming with Frost.*

Right now, though, climbing four flights of stairs seemed out of the question. Maybe he was sleepy? Maybe he should just close his eyes for a few moments and nap.

"Wadsworth."

He started. Callendra Brandish, the master of Gladius House, was standing in front of him, her arms crossed, a piece of her long brown hair loose from her ponytail and hanging down one side of her face.

Had he really fallen asleep? He hadn't heard her approach. She was dressed as if she were on her way to the faculty club for dinner—a nice dress and pearls—but somehow her raincoat over it all gave her the look of someone in priest's robes.

"Um, yes, Master Brandish?" His brain did a little flip at calling a woman "master," as it always did, even if she was as tall as most men. He supposed he would get used to it eventually.

"You don't look well," she said, narrowing her eyes as if she were examining a lab specimen.

"Oh, just tired," Kyle said and got to his feet, as if to prove he could. "I was just...taking a little nap before dinner."

She looked at her watch. "I think you need to eat as soon as possible. The dining hall doesn't open for another hour."

"Oh, I'm sure it's..."

"I know that sounded like a suggestion, Wadsworth, but it wasn't." She huffed impatiently, then dug in her purse for something. "Here. Eat this. Now."

Kyle took what she offered. A protein bar in shiny Mylar, one he could get from any convenience store. "Um, thanks, but..."

"That is an order, Wadsworth. I don't know what kind of hijinks you were up to today, but your energy is badly drained and if you don't replenish it quickly, the consequences can be quite serious." She glared until he tore the package open, then seemed to relax some. "If you're prone to this kind of energy drop, you may want to start carrying some of those bars yourself. They sell them at the drugstore in the Square."

He took a bite. It was crisped rice with a chocolate coating. The rest of it seemed to be something sort of like wall plaster, but it was surprisingly edible. "Um, thank you. Really. I feel better already."

Her look said: *No, you don't, but I'm polite enough that I won't call you on lying to me. This time.* "Give it a few minutes, and make sure you don't skip dinner either."

"Master, are you also, um, prone to energy drops?"

"No, I just have a tendency to get wrapped up in my work and forget to eat. Then I get cranky. And nobody likes me when I'm cranky."

"Er, no, of course not. Well, thank you again."

She nodded to him this time and walked out, the door to the vestibule making a gentle whooshing sound as she pushed it.

Kyle sat back down and finished the rest of the bar. He'd never been much prone to his blood sugar crashing before, but maybe he just hadn't really paid attention. Maybe he was going through a growth spurt. He hoped not. Having to replace all his pants again would be an expense he couldn't afford.

He took out his phone and text-messaged his Camella list. "Dinner at Scip in an hour? Starved. Meet me there."

Then he went upstairs to put his books away.

* * * *

An hour later he had already devoured a bourbon glazed pork loin, made a trip to the salad bar, and was just eyeing the make-your-own ice cream sundae stand when Alex and Jess strolled in together. They waved and got trays, getting food first before making their way over to him.

Jess kissed him on the cheek before settling down next to him. "Howdy, stranger," she said. "I haven't seen you all day."

"Nice to see you, too," he said. It wasn't at all unusual for them to go a day or even two without seeing anything of each other. They lived in different houses, they had no classes in common, and Kyle had been admonished already that he was expected to at least eat half his meals in his own dining hall.

What Kyle could not quite figure out was how often Jess expected to see him, or wanted to. She hadn't come out and said anything, but the way things had gone, they only went on a "date" on Fridays or Saturdays, and they only fooled around if they had had a date. He supposed it made sense; if they didn't limit themselves somehow, he could see how he could easily be convinced to just stay in bed all the time and only leave to go to class and meals.

When Alex had sat down, too, Kyle let out a long breath. "I need you guys to tell me everything about...about getting expelled or failed or whatever, and the Geas. I still don't understand what the Geas is."

Alex and Jess shared a look. Alex spoke first. "Why? I mean, sure, we'll tell you, but are you worried about something? You look worried, Kyle."

"Just something Frost said," he answered, his jaw clenching.

Alex made a dismissive noise. "You know better than to listen to him."

Jess put a hand on Kyle's forearm, although she kept eating her salad with the other hand. "The Geas is serious stuff. I mean, getting banished from the magical world, that's...that's pretty serious, but you have to take it seriously, too. There was a guy who was banished last year."

"There was?" Kyle felt a chill go through him.

"Yeah, we didn't know much about him. He was in Nummus, a grad student, wasn't he?" Alex frowned as he tried to remember. "Bah. We're even forgetting him already ourselves. It wasn't for academic failure, though. He'd breached secrecy somehow, right?"

Jess thought for a moment. "Something like that. Kyle, the thing is, the Geas is a really powerful spell that not only causes the person to forget all about us, but we start to forget them. It's really like they stop existing. Someone with the power to Judge, that's what they do. They change the fabric of our reality in some way. The only reason we remember anything at all about him is that we weren't really involved with him. The closer your connections to the person, the more quickly the forgetting reaches you. Only the Judges themselves remember."

Kyle wished he had gotten some more food before they had sat down. He settled for stealing cherry tomatoes out of Jess's salad. "So how does it work? I mean, is there a trial or something? And then they, what, wave a wand over you?"

Alex gave Jess a look, deferring to her. "It only takes one Judge to do it, but usually they get three together before making a decision," she said. "It's not like a normal court, though. The whole jury idea becomes useless when they can tell magically whether you are lying or not. It's not done in public, either. Just the accused, the accuser if there is one, and one to three judges."

Kyle shivered. "Do people know who the Judges are? Or is that a secret, too?"

Alex rolled his eyes. "If people didn't know who the Judges were, they couldn't accuse, could they? The main Judge for Veritas, of course is dean of the college, Dunster himself."

Jess snorted. "If he'd even deign to come down out of his ivory tower."

Kyle interrupted them. "You mean Quilian Bell isn't the dean?"

"Assistant dean," Alex said, his voice sharp with derision. "He runs everything because Dunster is supposedly in meditation most of the time. Handy that Bell's a Judge, too, so Dunster really never has to dirty his hands."

"Yeah. People see him maybe twice a year. Convocation and Commencement." She giggled. "Maybe he's a zombie."

Kyle's eyes were wide. "Are zombies real?"

Alex snorted. "No, they're not. Someone here's been watching too many bad movies lately."

"Sorry," Jess said with a last laugh behind her hand. "But seriously, how old is Dunster? Who was dean before him?"

Alex shrugged. "I don't know and I don't care."

"But I do." Kyle pushed his tray back. "About the Geas, I mean. So seriously all it would take is for some pissant like Frost to go to Bell and say 'Wadsworth's worthless and broke secrecy' and Bell could just zap me, like that?"

"Hey, hey, that's not what we said," Alex said, at the same time Jess said, "Oh, Kyle, it's not like that."

She continued. "You forget, the Judge wouldn't just be taking Frost's or whoever's word for it. They'd be able to test if he was lying. And bringing false accusation is nearly as bad a crime as breaking secrecy."

Alex stabbed at his pork loin. "*Did* Frost accuse you of something?"

Kyle shook his head. "No. But I'm really starting to worry about this not having an aptitude thing."

Jess patted his arm. "You've only been here a month, and you're cramming a million new things into your head. Give it time. No one is about to revoke your Magician's License."

"Li—?"

"She's kidding," Alex said pointedly. "I have something much more important to talk about."

"Which is?" asked Jess and Kyle at the same time.

"The Halloween Ball. What are you going to go as? I'm fresh out of ideas."

Jess shrugged. "Go to the costume place over by MIT and see if you like anything."

"Wait, are we supposed to dress up for this?" Kyle asked.

They both looked at him like he had just spoken ancient Aramaic. "It's Halloween, of course you're supposed to dress up," Alex said.

"But I would have thought that's mostly for...for the mundanes, right? Is all the stuff about the veil between worlds being thin really true, or is that just another story?"

"It is true," Jess said. "That's why you dress up. So if there's a ghost trying to haunt you, they won't find you."

"So...ghosts are real?" Kyle's voice was tentative this time.

"Of course ghosts are real," Jess said, annoyed.

"Well, how am I supposed to know?" Kyle got to his feet. "Ghost, zombies, werewolves, vampires...how the hell am I supposed to know the difference?"

He stomped off to the make-your-own-sundae bar, and immersed himself for several minutes in constructing a rather large thing with bananas around the edge, and chocolate and caramel sauce drizzled just so, and whipped cream, and jimmies.

When he got back to the table neither of them had moved. "Sorry," he said. "I didn't mean to be so...cranky." He thought of Master Brandish as he said that.

Maybe he'd feel better after the ice cream.

Jess's black eyes were fixed on him. "It's all right," she finally said. "It's just...it's hard for us to get used to how...um...clueless you are."

"Tactful, Jess, real tactful," Alex said with an amused air.

"Well, it's true! It's not like it's Kyle's fault he doesn't know anything, though. It's got to be like going to college in another country where you don't even speak the language or something."

Or you only speak the textbook version. We'll try to explain more and make fewer assumptions, Kyle. Won't we, Alex?"

Alex shrugged. "I'm not the one he yelled at."

"Who's yelling at who?" Randall sat down next to Alex. "Hey, Kyle. Got your text. Are they really getting you down over at Gladius House?"

Kyle groaned. "It's all formal manners and sitting in the pecking order over there. I can't believe I ended up there." He smacked his forehead. "If only I'd cut the cards! I would have gotten something else. But I was nervous, you know? I just kind of fumbled with the cards and took the one on top."

Jess stole a spoonful of his ice cream. "Well, no cut at all is still a kind of cut," she said. "And even if you *had* cut the cards, you still had a one in four chance of what you got being a sword, too, Kyle."

"But I don't feel like I belong there. I thought the whole point of the choosing was to get put where you belong?"

Alex took up a spoon and started stealing from Kyle's mountain of ice cream, too. "Well, the choosing doesn't always put you where you'd be happiest. And it sounds to me like you don't feel much like you belong anywhere right now."

"Well, that's true..."

"And who knows? Maybe fate has a reason for you to be there, Kyle." Randall looked around as he said this, as if worried about who might overhear. "Sometimes it takes time to see the design."

Alex ribbed him. "I thought you didn't believe in Soothsaying."

Randall drew himself up. "I never said that! I just don't believe I have any particular ability for it. Which my mother refuses to believe, but, well." He shrugged and began to placidly salt his food.

Randall had told Kyle during Alchemy last week that he was the first one in his family to attend Veritas. He came from a long line of voodoo practitioners in Trinidad, who all expected him to become the greatest Soothsayer of them all. He still hadn't told his mother he was planning to major in Alchemy, but he had a feeling she knew anyway, given the scolding tone of her recent letters and the number of luck talismans she had been sending.

A few more Camella folks came to sit with them after that. Kyle recognized Yoshi, a Japanese transfer student who hung around with them a lot and who seemed to have learned English from rap albums, and it looked like Jeanie and Lindy had brought Ciara, the Irish girl from poetry class.

Alex looked down the length of the table and then back at Kyle. "You feeling a little less lonely now, Ace?"

Kyle had to grin. "Yeah, I guess so."

"All right, so back to my original question. What are we going to wear for the Halloween Ball?"

* * * *

Kyle waited until Saturday night to try to talk to Jess about a lot of the things he had going through his head. They went to see a movie being shown on campus, but halfway through she squeezed his hand, they looked at each other, and he just knew they both wanted to go. So they left without saying a word, walking hand in hand past the cathedral-like edifice of Memorial Hall. Alex had taken him inside once just to see where the non-magical freshmen ate. "Like something right out of Oxford and Cambridge, isn't it?" he'd said. "The Ivy League had a real hard-on back in the days of the colonies to try to look and act as old as the old British colleges."

Now, as they made their way past it, Kyle said nothing, just gave Jess's hand another squeeze. They walked without a particular goal in mind, crossing the overpass by the firehouse into Harvard Yard, then out the other side into Harvard Square, bustling with Saturday night crowds enjoying the weather. The real winter cold would descend soon enough, or so everyone told him.

They ended up sitting on a bench in a small park not far from the Spanish restaurant where they'd eaten on Kyle's first day. A guy was playing guitar nearby, and from time to time someone on a skateboard would rattle past.

Kyle finally spoke when the song ended and the busker paused to chat with some passersby about his CD. "So, we're going to this ball, together, right? I mean, like you and me, together, not everyone in Camella 3 West."

Jess still hadn't let go of his hand and squeezed it gently. "If that's what you want."

"Of course it's what I want." He tried to tease out what could possibly be confusing about that, and yet it felt like there was a tangle. "Um, isn't it what you want?"

"I didn't want to presume," she said, eyes wide. "I mean, it's not like we're courting, right?"

"Courting?"

"You know what I mean. We're not dating so we can get engaged so we can get married." She cocked her head. "Are we?"

"I thought we were going to wait and see what happens." He felt like his voice got higher, but maybe it was just his heart sped up.

"Oh, yes." She put her other hand over their joined ones. "I guess what I'm trying to say, Kyle, is I didn't assume you wanted to go together like that. It's really sweet, though, that you assumed I would."

He felt like he was still missing something in what she was saying, a feeling that was all too familiar. The feeling that blanketed his days. All he could do, though, was forge ahead. "There's no one else for me, Jess. And I don't want there to be. I want it to be you and me, for as long as we both enjoy it. You and me...you know, like a couple."

Her smile was warm and open. "Okay. I didn't want to push you, what with you just getting settled here and all. I didn't assume that just because I was the first girl you met at Veritas, that I would be the only one you liked."

He laughed at that. "I was just lucky you were the first girl I met, because I would have been crazy about you anyway. Being in the right place at the right time, I got to know you immediately." He breathed a little easier and shifted to put an arm around her shoulders. "The rest, as they say, is history."

"Mm-hmm." She leaned her head against his shoulder with a happy sound, and he felt a wash of warm joy all the way down to his toes. The guy with the guitar began to play again.

"Maybe we should go to the ball as Zorro and...is there a female character in Zorro? I was trying to think of something Spanish," he said. He was actually trying to think of a character in a mask. What if this ball was Jess's dream come true? Wouldn't that be something?

She chuckled. "It'd be easy enough for me to go as generic señorita. But I'm not sure I'd want to. But you're right. We have to think of something or Alex will talk me, Lindy, and Jeanie into going as Charlie's Angels or something stupid like that."

"What about superheroes? Everyone could do whatever one they want, but then at least we'd sort of match."

"Who would you pick?"

"Hmm, good question. Batman would be kind of cool. You could totally do Wonder Woman if you wanted."

"Or Catwoman," she said with a sly tone in her voice. "Meowww."

Something about the way her voice dropped when she said "meow" sent his pulse throbbing through him. "Um, do you think we should head back?" he asked, trying to sound casual.

Her hand slid along the seam of his jeans at his inner thigh. "Oh, I don't know," she said in a singsong. "It's such a nice night..." Then her hand reached his zipper and she massaged him with the heel of her palm.

He pressed his lips to her hair, taking a slow breath of her scent. "It's a shame Brandish won't allow us to have visitors in our rooms." Well, visitors of the opposite sex. Kyle had run into Frost kissing his boyfriend in the stairwell plenty of times on their way to Frost's bed. "I have the place all to myself, after all."

Her wandering hand now made its way under his shirt and up his stomach. "My room's fine," she said. "Monica won't be back until late Sunday night or Monday morning."

Where does she go on the weekends, anyway? Kyle would have asked, but one of Jess's fingernails had found one of his nipples and that was apparently the off switch on his ability to speak.

"I wish I could carry you there right now," he said, when she let up. "Just pick you up and poof, be there in the blink of an eye."

She nuzzled under his chin. "That'd be more magical power than either of us have, you know. And when we got there, we'd be too tired to do anything."

"Guess we'll have to walk, then."

She nibbled for a moment on his earlobe before getting to her feet.

* * * *

Once the door was closed behind them, Kyle bent her into a kiss, a real kiss. They never did this in public, tongues seeking each other and neither of them able to hold back the hungry noises they made. It thrilled Kyle suddenly to realize they'd kissed like this enough times now that he could no longer keep count of them.

They had gotten good at undressing while kissing. Kyle had taken to always wearing shirts with buttons since they didn't have to be pulled over his head and he couldn't help but notice that she often did the same. He freed her shoulders of her shirt and undid the clasp of her bra in front, his thumbs finding her nipples before the bra could fall away. It felt like as the two nubs came to full hardness they sent an instant message to his cock to do the same.

He felt her hands slide over his ass as she eased his jeans down, then quite suddenly he was bereft of her as she broke the kiss and seemed to disappear. He opened his eyes to find she had dropped to her knees to bring his underwear all the way to his ankles, and then she stayed down there, looking up at him and cupping his balls with one hand.

She licked her lips and he was reminded of the cat noise she'd made before, the association even stronger as she began licking his erection like a cat grooming its paw. Her eyes closed as she did it, but he stared, soaking in every moment of the incredible image. When she closed her lips over the head and then gently sucked the entire thing in deeper, he nearly fell over.

"I don't...think my knees are going to hold out," he said, trying to catch his breath.

She pulled off his cock with a wet pop. "Bed, then." She shooed him over to it and he sat, then lay down at her urging gestures. She shed the rest of her clothes, her panties and a pair of socks, and crawled over him, settling down so her belly slid against his saliva-slick cock. She ground upward, her hips undulating slowly, until he moaned, then she moved down between his legs to take him in her mouth again.

She had convinced him quite thoroughly that for purposes of Esoteric Studies, virginity was too significant to be given up just for the sake of recreational enjoyment. There were strict definitions of what losing one's virginity meant. Oral sex was apparently okay. So was rubbing your genitals against your partner until you came, or letting them rub you with their fingers.

Kyle had always let Jess lead their lovemaking since she knew the rules, and also since she had a bit more experience; she knew what she wanted and what to try. Not that he didn't think up things, but she seemed happy and eager to lead, so he figured he'd hold his ideas in reserve in case Jess was ever at a loss for what to do next. Some of the time what he thought of, she would think of herself soon after, which just proved to him, as their comfortable silence and their mutual moment of "let's go" had, that they were a perfect match for each other.

She climbed back up to lie next to him in the narrow bed when his legs began to shake like his orgasm was imminent. He turned to kiss her mouth, her lips so full and red from the friction against his cock, the flavor salty like sweat. She guided his hand to her mound and he let his fingers part her lips, seeking out first her slippery juices and smearing them upward over her clit, the way she had taught him to that first night together.

He held her spread and flicked his middle finger lightly over the slick nub until her hips began to jerk, when he knew he could apply more pressure. In a matter of just a few minutes, she had trapped his hand between her thighs and was jerking hard in the throes of her orgasm. He had also learned not to pull away or to stop sawing at her clit until she said to, since sometimes a second and a third orgasm followed hot on the heels of the first.

At last she opened those obsidian black eyes and looked at him through a haze of lust. "Come here," she said, shifting more onto her back and pulling him so that he was on top of her. She trapped his cock in the sticky crux of her legs, so very close to the forbidden place that his breath caught and his arms trembled as he held himself up.

"Like that," she said, pulling at his buttocks, until his hips were a little closer to her head than her own, angling his cock over her clit and into the grip of her thighs.

"Isn't this dangerous?" he asked, voice rough with lust.

"I trust you, Kyle." She craned her neck upward to place a kiss on his chin. "If you want to be sure, when you get really close, pull up and rub off against my hip or stomach, okay?"

"Okay." This wasn't just about magic, but about potential pregnancy, wasn't it? He was pretty sure they'd said in ninth-grade sex ed class that it wasn't a good idea to ejaculate any-where near the vagina. Better safe than sorry.

He began to thrust into the wet warmth between her thighs and they both moaned. And real sex supposedly felt even better than this? At the moment, he couldn't believe that.

He nearly lost it when she began to come again, and gripped onto his cock the way she always did his hand, but he managed to hold back until she let go, and he just got his cock pressed against her stomach when hot come spurted out of him.

"Merlin and Morgana's goat-fucking third cousin," he said, choosing one of Alex's more colorful swears for the occasion. "You are in-fucking-credible."

She laughed and pulled him down for a kiss. "Now you're starting to sound like one of us."

"Good." He settled next to her so he wouldn't crush her and realized he felt content for the first time in days. "You're amaz-ing. You're everything I could dream." The words *I love you* hov-ered behind his teeth, too, but he held onto them. He wanted to wait to say them when he knew he really meant them, not when he was giddy from sex and would say almost anything.

"You're amazing, too, Kyle," she said, reaching behind her pillow for a towel. She wiped them both up and then tossed the towel aside, pulling up a blanket instead. "You're not going anywhere for a while?"

"Not unless you want to kick me out."

"Uh-uh." She pulled him close and they fell asleep like that, arms entwined.

* * * *

Upon hearing that Jess and Kyle were going to go to the ball as Batman and Catwoman, Alex declared that he would not go as Robin the Boy Wonder and that it was now Kyle's job to help him find something. Thus it was that on Saturday, Kyle found himself on the T with his friend, riding to Kendall Square. They emerged on the edge of the MIT campus and then walked several blocks, passing office towers for biotech and research companies until they came to a squat little brick warehouse.

"The Garment District?" Kyle read off the sign, hand-painted on the brick.

Alex led Kyle through a narrow door into the store.

Kyle stopped and took in the view a few steps into the place. The ground floor had a costume shop off to one side, and what looked like the world's largest laundry pile on the other. Several people, mostly women, were climbing carefully through the pile, examining the clothes one piece at a time.

Alex shrugged in that direction. "They sell all that stuff by the pound. Dollar-fifty a pound, I think? Upstairs is the biggest secondhand clothing store I've ever seen. But this is what we want." He led Kyle into the costume area. One whole wall section was covered with wigs. Several fancy costumes hung from hangers on pegs: a pirate, a space alien, a Kiss-like rock-and-roll outfit.

"If you want to match, you could always go as The Joker or something," Kyle suggested as they began to look through a book of costumes on the counter.

"Ha, ha, very funny," Alex said.

"Is something wrong?" Kyle had never heard Alex quite so moody.

"Oh just, you know, no one believes I take anything seriously, so, of course, The Joker." He flipped the pages disinterestedly.

"That isn't what I meant at all." Kyle frowned. "But you *do* give the impression that you don't take anything seriously, you know."

"I know." Alex fell silent, closing the book and moving to a rack to browse through some outfits.

Kyle tagged along. He had already gotten his costume—a cheap-ass drugstore model, but it would do. The mask was the important thing, he figured.

He'd also tried writing a poem for Jess. He imagined they would get hot and thirsty from dancing, and they would take a break, walking away from the noise and energy of the dance floor into somewhere cool and quiet and shadowed, and then he would recite his poem, words that would finally make clear to her how he truly felt. Her dream would come true, and so would his. Happily ever after.

Except that every poem he'd tried to write this week had been utter drivel.

Maybe I should just find one of Longfellow's...? But reciting the work of another, even a vaunted ancestor, wasn't the same. *Inspiration will come. It will.*

He tried again with Alex. "There are plenty of other heroes or villains to choose from, you know."

"Yeah, I know."

"The Riddler? Mr. Freeze? Spiderman?"

"I don't want a costume that hides my face and hair."

"Okay, Superman? Um, Wonder Woman?"

Alex let out a laugh. "Cross-dressing is a time-honored tradition for this holiday, after all...and let me tell you, I look great in fishnet stockings."

"Ugh, I'm not sure I needed that image in my head."

Alex pulled out something on a hanger. "Hmm. Maybe I could pull off a pirate. Not the fancy kind like Captain Morgan or something, but more...yeah. I could put a hoop in my ear and borrow a parrot." Kyle followed Alex up to the second floor, where Alex proceeded to spend the next hour hunting out the perfect shirt, breeches, headscarf, sash belt, and so on from the racks and rack and racks of clothing on display there. Even better, when he was done, he paid under $20 for his acquisitions. Kyle was amazed.

"Finding a bargain...finding just about anything, is one of my aptitudes," Alex explained when they were on their way down the stairs. When they reached the street, Kyle turned to the right back toward the train, but Alex said, "You hungry? My aptitude says there's something delicious this direction." He pointed the opposite way.

"Um, sure."

They walked further up the street, where it turned residential, trees lining the curbs in front of wooden houses built in Victorian times.

"So are you being serious?" Kyle pressed, as they turned down a side street. "About finding things?"

Alex shrugged. "Yeah. It's a tricky one, though. Doesn't always work, just like how soothsaying is on and off for most people."

"If your aptitude is on and off," Kyle said, "then how do you figure out what you're doing is magic?"

"Well, if you're making something levitate, or things appear out of thin air, it probably doesn't take more than once or twice for you to be convinced. But subtler things...you know how they say third time's the charm? If you do something three times, it really starts to seem for real, doesn't it?"

"I wouldn't know," Kyle said, a little glumly.

"Buck up, Ace, you'll figure it out." Alex punched him lightly on the arm. "Let's talk about something more cheerful. Like... how you and Jess are doing."

Kyle's laugh was wry. "We're doing well."

"But? I can hear a 'but' there."

It was Kyle's turn to shrug. "But I don't think she takes me seriously. I mean, not as seriously as I take her. She's great, she's wonderful to me. The time we spend together is amazing." He blushed a little but knew Alex already was privy to what their sex life was like. "We never fight, and every time I see her I just get more and more into her."

"That's how she was with me when we dated for like two months last year. Really fun to be around, seemed to like me plenty, but..."

"But what?"

"But I got out before I got sucked in any deeper, because I knew I wasn't 'the one' for her."

"The one?"

"Don't you get the feeling you're just a...an appetizer, while she's waiting for the main course?"

Huh. Maybe Alex had the aptitude for picking the right words. "Yeah, that's exactly how I feel. I...I kind of hope things change at the ball, though."

"Oh?" Now Alex was looking at him as they walked, curiosity at full burn.

"Well, yeah. Okay, here's why. She told me she had a dream she's going to meet her true love at a costume party. I feel like, well, this is falling right into my lap. How can I not grab the chance?"

"Hmm. Well, Fate is like that sometimes." Alex pushed open the front door on a restaurant that looked like a house. Inside, there was a counter to order food from, and a few small tables scattered around. A radio was playing some kind of Spanish music. One portion of the menu seemed to be regular submarine sandwiches, but all the rest, as Alex explained it, pointing to the lists of dishes posted above the counter, was Puerto Rican food.

"Is that like Mexican food?" Kyle asked.

"No. Not really. How hungry are you? I'll order. Go snag a table."

Kyle took a seat near the door, while Alex talked for a while with the man behind the counter, then came and sat down. What came next was a steady stream of food served up on Styrofoam plates. Thin seared steak with rice and beans and fried bananas. A bowl of goat stew. Some kind of little doughy meat pies.

And somehow, again, the bill came to under $20.

When they were nearly back at the train, stomachs completely full and the prospect of a mid-afternoon nap looming, Kyle asked, "So that was really the price, right? You didn't put the whammy on them or something?"

Alex's voice was scathing. "The. Whammy."

"You know what I mean!"

Alex laughed, relenting. "You mean, did I use the Jedi Mind Trick to get them to undercharge us?"

"Yeah."

"No. No, I didn't. They're both just dirt-cheap places." He started down the stairs to the train platform.

"So that's just one of those things that only happens in fairy tales?"

"I didn't say that."

"You mean you really could do something like that?"

"Kyle, Kyle, Kyle, you're going to have to learn to speak more precisely. It's exactly that kind of sloppy jumping to conclusions that leads mundanes into trouble in all the stories, isn't it?" Alex chuckled to himself. "It's too bad the train is automated now. I don't have the touch with machines that I do with people. I could always talk my way on when there were human attendants. Oh, shit, here it comes..."

He jumped down the last two steps and went through the gate while Kyle was still fumbling to get his wallet out of his pocket. He pressed it against the reader pad and the gate swung open to let him through as well.

He looked up at Alex, who was standing at the yellow line, waiting for the train's doors to open. Had he really gotten his transit card out? Kyle had been busy with his own, so maybe he had and Kyle had missed it.

Alex gave him a sly half smile and stepped into the car.

* * * *

The night before the ball, Kyle was getting desperate. Poem after poem turned out to be junk. Jess had even been the one who told him love potions didn't work, but that love poems did. Had she been sort of asking him to try it? He tore up a whole page of flower and fruit metaphors. Finally he decided that he needed a break and he made his way down to the Gladius dining hall, where around ten o'clock each night, they would put out snacks for those staying up late to study.

He was nearly knocked down in the doorway by someone trying to leave the room in great haste, someone with silk-straight black hair and glasses. He just barely dodged Michael Candlin, Frost's boyfriend, as he escaped.

Kyle stepped cautiously into the room to see Frost on his feet at one end of a table, as if he'd just stood, and Master Brandish making herself a cup of tea at the hot drinks stand. A few students sat against the back wall.

Kyle made his way to the snack display, where chocolate chip cookies—some of them laced with M&Ms—were laid out, still slightly warm. He put three into a napkin, took a small carton of milk, and made as if to leave.

"Wadsworth."

Kyle stopped in front of the table where Frost had seated himself again. "Frost." He had a feeling the House Master was watching them, but didn't dare turn to look.

"Found an aptitude yet?" Frost arched one jet black eyebrow.

"Figured out what you're wearing to the ball yet?" Kyle shot back, a weak rejoinder but mostly he just wanted to be out of this conversation as quickly as possible.

Frost snorted. "There are much better things to do on All Hallow's Eve than dance around in a stupid costume," he said. "Especially if you're trying to tap into your as-yet-unreached well of power."

"What are you talking about?"

"Isn't that girlfriend of yours a Ritual Arts major? Ask her. She'll no doubt have some suggestions."

Jess *was* actually angling towards Healing Arts and hadn't declared yet, but Kyle didn't say that. *I can't whine to Jess any more about being a late bloomer. Right now I don't want her focused on my faults and deficiencies.* "Well, and how are you going to be spending the holiday?"

"Why don't you meet me on the roof of William James Hall at ten o'clock and find out?" Frost's blue eyes glittered.

"I've already got a date, thanks," Kyle shot back.

"Oh ho. Well. Bring her." Frost got to his feet and picked up his tray. He passed very close to Kyle as he went to dump out his trash. Kyle could have sworn that when they met, they were the same height, but now he couldn't see the top of Frost's head. It did seem Frost liked to act bigger than those around him; maybe he wore platform shoes?

Frost left the room. Kyle could still hear the clinking of Master Brandish's teaspoon in her mug and knew she had been watching the entire scene.

Kyle hurried out as well before anything else could go wrong.

* * * *

On Halloween morning, he received a letter from Great-Aunt Agatha.

Dearest Kyle, it began, which he couldn't help but hear in an ironic tone. Very little was dear to Agatha other than her very old, half-blind tomcat Mr. Whiskers, and her attic full of old furniture and junk.

I hope you are doing well at Harvard. I still do not know what to tell the neighbors about your sudden departure as your explanation about the professor in immediate need of a fellowship student assistant is still very plainly hogwash to me, young man, and so I am loath to repeat it. I have been instead acting as if they are the ones who are confused. "What? You knew Kyle was accepted to Harvard, didn't you? Oh yes, didn't you realize it was this year he was going?" That of course works with many, but there are those who would think I have gone out of my mind except for the fact that you are very definitely Not In Evidence. Therefore I must either be telling the truth or I've hidden your body somewhere. I resent greatly that you have put me in this position, and I would at least appreciate something from you that I can show them that a normal college freshman would send to his family. I am enclosing twenty dollars in case that should help.

"Jeez, Agatha, I can tell you really miss me, too," he said sarcastically. What did the neighbors think? First Jove, then Kyle? He doubted the neighbors even noticed. He nearly crumpled up the letter, but instead took the twenty dollars down to the Coop and bought a shirt that said "Harvard" in large letters across the top, centered over the shield-like logo reading VE-RI-TAS. He then spent an hour trying to take pictures of himself on the steps of Widener Library with his cell phone camera and mostly failing until he saw Yoshi coming out of the library.

"Yosh! Can you help me?"

"What up, dog?" Yoshi always sounded to Kyle like nearly everything he said was a question. Something about his accent and the way his eyebrows went up and made his eyes seem very wide and inquisitive. Yoshi seemed to aspire to the "cool" of a pop star, his clothes often looking like something straight from a music video, but his face never managed the pouty disdain or artful smolder that would match.

"I'm trying to take a picture of myself to print out and send to my great aunt to prove I'm really at Harvard." Kyle handed him the phone with the camera set to go.

Yoshi examined the camera. "You need megapixels! Use mine?" He pulled a phone out of his jacket pocket.

"Okay, but hurry." Kyle rubbed his bare arms. It was a bit chilly to be standing out there without a jacket.

Yoshi backed down several steps, then Kyle heard the sound effect of a camera shutter and was surprised to even see a flash.

Yoshi hurried back up to show him the results on a screen much larger and clearer than the one on Kyle's crappy phone. "You look awesome? Very cool. Very fly, my man. E-mail?"

"Um, sure. Yeah, that works."

Kyle pulled his jacket back on and thanked Yoshi for the help, then headed off to one of the places on campus he could get the file and print it. He wondered if perhaps he could return the shirt now and get the money back—trying to stretch his unspent book stipend to last to the end of the semester was already going to be a challenge, but in the end he decided he liked the shirt. An hour later he had printed the photo nicely, and mailed it in a nice envelope with a brief letter which said nothing of consequence.

He was sure Agatha would take one look at it, then probably never take it out of the envelope again. Her mantel was covered with photos of other family members, and she even had one of Jove, but in all the time Kyle had lived with her, she'd never put up one of him.

Whatever. Agatha was in the past. In the present, he still had a poem to write.

* * * *

Putting on his costume alone in his room, Kyle wondered if maybe he should have gone over to Camella House and gotten dressed with the rest of them. Then maybe he wouldn't be turning back and forth in front of the mirror wondering whether the entire thing looked remarkably stupid.

The weather was too cold to just wear the costume as it was, so he'd put a shirt on under it, but then it looked too bulky, so he had taken it off again. The tights for his legs were so thin, it felt like the breeze was blowing right up his ass crack, honestly. It was a little better with the cape and cowl on, though. Maybe it would be all right. It would be kind of dark in the dance hall anyway, and he decided he had just better stop worrying about it. He was committed to this course of action.

He was meeting Jess in the front of Lowell House, one of the non-magical residential houses. The Lowell dining hall was large enough to host a dance for a few hundred people, something none of the magical houses could boast. Kyle wondered if it could be a problem, having a bunch of magical revelers in a building where so many mundanes lived, but then they shared classroom buildings every day and no one seemed to blink.

The sun had set, but it didn't seem too cold just yet.

Lindy and Jeanie came up to him, holding hands. Kyle attempted not to blink or look shocked—had he known they were a couple? Or was it part of their costuming for the night? Lindy was wearing a black wig and was dressed like a belly dancer, while Jeanie looked...sort of like a geisha, maybe?

"Wow, Kyle, impressive package," Jeanie said, then reddened, her hand over her mouth, while Lindy laughed.

"Yeah, nice tights," she added.

"Um, you guys are..."

Jeanie uncovered her mouth. "You really have no idea, do you?"

"I'm Jasmine, she's Mulan. We convinced Marjory to come as Cinderella, have you seen her? And Marigold is going to be Snow White, and Kate... I can't remember who Kate was going to be." Lindy tapped her finger against her pursed lips.

"Ariel?" Jeanie guessed. "What other Disney princesses are there?"

"Oh, right. I think she decided on Pocahontas, though. And Monica was going to do Ariel since she doesn't like dancing that much."

Monica was Jess's roommate, whom Kyle almost never saw since Jess always planned his visits to coincide with her absence. He nodded like he'd known all along what their common theme was—somehow Disney princesses wouldn't have probably been high on his list. Then again, what other common theme could he come up with that could accommodate so many girls? He wondered if Jess felt left out. "I haven't seen Marjory yet, but I've only been standing here for a few minutes. Did you guys see Jess?"

"She was already gone when we left, I think?" Lindy said, looking around. "She might have come here with her costume to change into it here. I think that's what Marjory was planning to do. Maybe they're together."

Marjory was the resident tutor on the Camella House third floor. Kyle had met her a few times in passing. She was a grad student in Esoteric Studies, but he didn't know her well. Jess talked about her some because Marjory was someone she had spoken with a lot regarding which major to pick.

"Oh. My. God." Lindy's eyes were wide, looking at someone over Kyle's shoulder.

Kyle turned quickly, his cape swirling, and caught sight of a woman in black stiletto boots and a skintight black suit, carrying a bullwhip. She had a panther-like slink to her walk, hips rolling, and a black mask around her eyes, and...

Oh. And cat ears. "Jess?"

"Rrrrrow," she said as she came close, running one fingernail under Kyle's chin. "Shall we go in?"

"Sure." He followed her, turning back to give a half-hearted wave to the other two. They were giggling as they waved back.

Inside the hall, colorful lights had been set along the walls, painting them in gold and purple and green and blue, and from time to time the colors changed with the music. All the dining tables had been removed, leaving a large open floor with a deejay at one end. Kyle didn't recognize the song playing, but it had a nice beat to it and Jess pulled him right out onto the dance floor. There were already a few dozen people dancing while others stood around the edges watching, or walked back and forth between the various snack and drink stations set up in the corners.

But Kyle only took that in at the edges of his vision. Jess filled his sight, and he wanted nothing more than to just run his hands down the sleek gloss of her hair, over the skintight curves of her outfit, pulling her against him.

Instead, they danced, which was dizzying and made his blood rush nearly as much. She came close enough sometimes for him to catch her scent, but she wasn't touching him. He felt the edge of his cape swishing along the backs of his legs and wondered what she would say if he picked her up and tried to carry her. Although Camella House was probably too far for that.

Those were the sorts of thoughts that ran through his head, and just as he was beginning to wonder how much time had passed, and whether maybe they ought to pause to get drinks, the music slowed.

He didn't hesitate, pulling her close as the slow dance began. She sighed contentedly as she leaned her head against his, nearly his height in her tall boots. Kyle was anything but content, but his instincts were soothed for the moment. Closer was better than not closer, after all. He lost himself in the scent of her shampoo, and decided when the song ended, he'd ask if she wanted to get some air.

His reverie was broken by someone tapping on his shoulder, and a voice, "May I cut in?"

"Um, sure..." he said automatically, before he realized who it was.

But a moment later Frost was in his arms, his wrists crossed behind Kyle's head. "Frost, what...?" He looked up and saw Candlin was dancing with Jess, who had to look down at him from her high heels.

Frost leaned close. "It's nearly half past nine, you know? Don't be late."

Then just as suddenly, his arms were empty and Frost was making his way toward the exit. The music changed, picking up pace, and Jess was chuckling as Candlin bowed to her and left her, too.

She seized Kyle's hand as she pushed him toward the edge of the dancing. "So," she said, once they were a bit further from the deejay and the speakers. "Are we going to the broom race?"

"Um, what?"

"Michael said Frost invited us to go."

"Oh." Kyle blinked. "Er, yeah. Roof of William James Hall, ten o'clock. Do you want to go?"

She grinned. "I've never been! It's usually only the Gladius types who get to go."

So Frost wasn't calling him out for a duel or trying to hit on him or any of the other quick mental explanations Kyle had come up with for the secret rendezvous. Or not so secret, as it turned out. "Wait a minute. They actually race brooms?" Kyle asked, his curiosity getting the better of his usual instinct to just play along and try to fit in.

"So I hear. Come on." She led the way out of the hall, drawing a few appreciative whistles from some of their compatriots.

Kyle followed, starting to wonder if he really should have brought a coat. The roof of the tallest building on the campus was not likely to be a warm and cozy place. Maybe they could stop at Gladius House and he could pick one up? But, no. He couldn't see himself complaining in front of her. So he kept his mouth shut as they crossed the campus, the clouds shredding like gossamer to reveal a gibbous moon a third of the way up the sky.

* * * *

He wasn't surprised to find a door to the building "conveniently" unlocked, nor another one leading to the roof stairwell.

He was surprised to see Alex, squatting on the gravel roof with two guys Kyle didn't recognize, passing a pipe back and forth between them. Alex was in his pirate outfit, though he'd lost his headscarf somewhere along the way, and a parrot—a real, live parrot—was pecking at the gravel near his boots.

About twenty other students were there, and Kyle found himself looking for Frost among them. The shadows were strange and disorienting, the light coming from two corners of the roof. He couldn't tell if it was always like that, or if the students had rigged the lights. Jess held his hand, which was the only warm part of him up here in the wind. She pulled him closer to the edge and they looked down on Memorial Hall in all its cathedral glory. He put his arms around her as if to warm her up, and wondered if his shivering was too obvious.

"I wonder if someone brought...aha. Come on." She pulled him closer to a small knot of people where a Gladius House tutor, Remy, was passing out tiny glass vials from his messenger bag. Jess went and got two, bringing them back to Kyle.

"What is it?" He held it up in the light and saw it was a deep red color like wine.

Jess had already downed hers. "You'll be warm once you drink it."

"Will you tell me what it is if I drink it?"

She giggled as he pulled the cork and drank, then answered, "It's magic."

It was. He felt the warmth start in his stomach and blossom outward, almost like getting goose bumps, except it was heat that flashed over his skin when it reached there. The palms of his hands were suddenly hot.

"They call it Red Heat. If you end up going any further in Alchemy, you might learn to make it," she said, watching his stunned expression. Then she slid into his arms. For a moment he thought it might feel too hot to be in such close contact— but no, after the initial flash, the effect seemed to mellow to a steady warmth that felt even better when they were holding each other.

Remy whistled and the crowd quieted down. He was a stout upperclassman, his sandy hair overgrown like he'd just not gotten around to trimming it, and he was wearing a blue jacket with the Gladius House crest on the breast pocket. Now Kyle could see Frost, standing next to Remy and holding what looked like a broom he'd just pulled from a closet somewhere in one hand. Behind him stood three others with brooms, two guys and a girl. Kyle recognized them all as upperclassmen in Gladius House.

The ones with brooms were all dressed in dark clothing, and Kyle wondered how they were supposed to be able to see them against the dark sky, even with the moon as it was. His answer came soon enough. One by one, each of them took something from Remy that looked like an Olympic medal and put it over their heads. Then they each began to glow: Frost, blue; the one he recognized as Caitlyn Speyer, red; and the other two, green and yellow. The reflected light made Candlin's glasses look opaque.

Weren't they just fighting? Kyle thought. Whatever had caused Candlin to storm out of the dining hall seemed to be done with now, anyway.

The racers lined up on the edge of the roof, facing Harvard Yard. Alex and some of the others hoisted a tall pole into the air, atop which flew a strip of white ribbon. "Round one!" Remy declared. "Around the steeple of Memorial Church and back. First one to grab the ribbon is the winner!" He rang a bell and Kyle's heart jumped into his throat as all four racers dove from the ledge, dropping out of sight. It was only a fraction of a second, though, before four streaking comets shot upward toward the white spire they could clearly see from this vantage point. They had been fairly closely bunched, but somehow during the turn around the steeple, Speyer and the green racer had gotten entangled, and Frost and the other were in the clear lead on the way back.

They were neck and neck, hands outstretched toward the target, waving in the wind, two blurs of colored light shooting overhead. The whoop of triumph that came down wasn't Frost's voice, though.

That came a few seconds later. "I'll get you on the next round, Allan!"

Allan, Kyle now remembered, was supposedly related to none other than Poe, but he usually tried to block out the dining room gossip and so wasn't sure whether it was true. All four racers soon made their landings, the other three at high speed, coming to stumbling stops, Frost more slowly and alighting with a few gentle jogging steps.

They reassembled at the edge. Another ribbon was hoisted, this one either brown or red—Kyle wasn't sure in the light.

"Round two!" Remy barked, the wind blowing his hair across his eyes. "All the way to the river! Under the Kennedy Street bridge! And back to grab the ribbon! Marks...go!" He rang the bell again. This time Kyle was prepared for the leap of the racers and saw them wrap their legs around the broom handles before their speed turned them to blurs again.

When they were out of sight, he whispered to Jess. "So what makes the brooms fly?"

"It's a combination of the amulets they are wearing, the conditioning on the brooms, and their own inherent magic," she said. "The keepers of the brooms are all in Gladius House. You'd have a better chance of finding out exactly how they do it than I would."

"What do you mean conditioning?"

"There are certain kinds of spells you can do, like soaking the wood with the essence of certain flowers, only under the full moon on a cloudless night...that sort of thing. I'm under the impression it takes all year to get the brooms ready...oh, here they come again."

Speyer was in the lead this time, and Kyle could hear her laughter as she closed in on the target, grabbing the ribbon and circling them once quickly before the other three arrived.

"Aren't they kind of conspicuous? Glowing like that?" Kyle asked, settling his arms around Jess from behind so he could keep whispering into her ear, hold her, and they could both face the racers.

"Only if you have the Sight," Jess answered. "And look up at the right time."

"Round three!" Remy cleared his throat to quiet the well wishers around Caitlyn, then tried again. "Round three. The distance round! All the way to the tower at Powderhouse Circle, then back to ring the bell on the Swedenborg Chapel, around the spire of the First Church, then back here for the final ribbon!"

Once again the racers dropped away, this time veering to the right as soon as they were off, and disappearing over the buildings of the law school.

"Pretty neat, huh?" Alex said.

Jess startled. "When did you get there?"

"Just now," he said with a chuckle. The parrot made an affirmative whistling noise. "Isn't that right, Corky?" He gave the parrot some kind of nut or seed and the parrot went to work happily on opening it. "Been a long time since I raced a broom."

Kyle's ears perked up. "I really want to try it."

Alex shrugged, scanning the sky in the direction the racers had gone. "After the three races, there's not a lot left, usually, but they will let folks fly around a little until they go dry. You just have to be careful that you aren't flying over the river or a major street when you run out. The broom will get lower and lower so by the time it does you won't have far to fall."

Kyle nodded, but sighed inwardly. This seemed to be largely a Gladius House tradition, and if it was like other house traditions, Kyle was too far down the pecking order to rate a flight before the brooms would be exhausted. Maybe next year.

"Here they come!" Jess pointed. A blue comet was in the lead, no sound coming from Frost at all as he struck the bell and reversed direction, Caitlyn only a second or two behind, then Allan. All the ending landmarks were visible from here, and the students crowded along the edge. Frost was nearly at the First Church when the murmuring began. "Where's Nichols?"

The fourth racer was not visible yet. Meanwhile in making the next turn, Frost lost a fraction of a second; then it was him and Speyer. Both whipped past overhead so quickly, Kyle could not tell who had won until Frost came fluttering down with the last ribbon, a lovely deep purple shade, entwined in his fingers. He kissed Candlin upon touching down, and draped the ribbon over his shoulders.

"What's wrong?" he asked, a hand on Candlin's upper arm.

"Nichols hasn't come in," Remy said. Two students with binoculars were scanning the sky in the direction of Powderhouse Circle.

"Oh for the love of..." Frost went directly to the edge and leaped, even as Remy reached out a hand to stop him.

"Crazy-ass maniac!" Remy shouted after him. "Now we'll probably end up with both of them stranded in Somerville somewhere."

"Give him a break, Rem." Caitlyn took off her amulet and the glow around her faded, darkening her naturally red hair. "If he finds him, the broom's the quickest way to get him back here."

"Or maybe he just didn't want to give it up." Remy took her amulet and the broom, then went to collect the others.

"What do you...?" Kyle started to ask Alex something, but Alex was not standing where he had been a minute before. He shook his head and asked Jess instead. "Will they be okay, you think?"

"Yeah, probably," Jess said. "Nichols probably ran out of gas early for some reason—either his broom just didn't have enough, or he wasn't channeling his energy well..."

"Hey, Kyle!"

Kyle looked up to see Alex waving to him from the edge of the building with a broom in his hand. "Come here and try this!"

Kyle and Jess exchanged a look. "Go on, " she said. "You know you want to."

He hurried over to Alex who urged him to take the mask and cape off. "We can both go. Stand in front of me and put the broom through our legs like this..." Alex pulled him close with one arm. "Then the amulet's ribbon needs to go around both our heads." A student Kyle didn't know put the amulet on them. "Okay, Ace, you ready for this?"

"Won't we weigh twice as much?" Kyle asked, a little nervous.

"And won't we have twice the magical power a single person has?" Alex countered.

"Um, yeah," Kyle said, but in his head he was thinking, *What if I don't have any magical power after all? What if I'm just one of those Sighted weirdos? What if we fall off this building and die?*

But then there wasn't any more thinking to be done because Alex jumped them both off the building. Kyle felt his stomach hit the roof of his mouth, but then he opened his eyes because it didn't feel like they were plummeting to their deaths. It felt like they were soaring.

"Pretty cool, huh?" Alex said, in his ear. "Just keep your knees together."

"Okay." The warming draught they'd taken before was still at work, and where Alex pressed against his back and where his arm held around Kyle's middle felt almost tingling with heat. The rush of the wind on his face was delightful as they flew over the Yard, right past Kyle's own window at the top of Gladius House, then turned in a wide arc to head back. Kyle laughed as he realized Alex's green parrot was flying alongside them.

"We'll come in as slow as we can. Let the momentum carry you into a run," Alex said as they approached the roof. Kyle thought of how Frost had done a little jog.

Their landing wasn't perfect, as they tripped each other up a little, and only quick thinking by Alex saved Kyle from being choked by the amulet, but as Kyle ended up falling into Jess's arms, he counted the maneuver a success. The broom was passed on to someone else.

"Thanks, Alex." Kyle realized his heart was still pounding from the adrenaline rush. "That was really something."

"No problem, Ace." Alex whistled and the parrot came back to his shoulder. "You guys heading back to the dance?"

"I think we had enough dancing," Jess said, her hand sliding down Kyle's hip.

"Ahh. I see. Well, you kids have fun." Alex gave them a little wave and then headed over to some other students, pulling the pipe from a pocket somewhere and waving it enticingly. From overhead came a joyful laugh, and Kyle looked up to see another pair go by on the other broom, waving to them.

"Do you want to stay and watch more?" Jess asked. "I'm not sure how many more flights there will be."

Kyle smiled. "I've seen plenty now."

They were just heading for the stairwell when a shout went up. "Here they come!"

The blue glow that was Frost was getting larger and larger, but also seemed dangerously low to the rooftops. The yellow flicker of Nichols was overlapping as if Frost were carrying him. The yellow glow also did not seem very strong compared to earlier. "Oh shit," Jess said.

"They're coming down!"

Frost and Nichols had just cleared the roof of the physics building and were losing altitude, heading for the circle of grass in the driveway of Memorial Hall. Kyle found himself in the front of the group racing down the stairs, trying to get to them as quickly as possible. Halfway down, he wondered where Jess was. Had she been left behind because of her high heels? He couldn't stop now, though, or the people racing down behind him would run smack into him.

They burst out of the doors on the first floor and ran across Kirkland Street, and as Kyle got closer he saw Jess was already there, with Remy and Speyer each of them holding a broom. Jess was kneeling at Nichols's head, her palms against his temples, her eyes closed. Frost was sitting next to her, looking as pale and drained as ever.

Jess began to chant in a language Kyle didn't recognize, as the students formed a circle all the way around them. Only now did Kyle make out a large bruise on Nichols's forehead, the spot swelling up badly. Jess's hands moved over his forehead and her chant stopped as she bowed her head. All of them were silent, the hiss of traffic going to and from Oxford Street the only sound.

Kyle was startled as Jess suddenly threw her hands in the air with a kind of anguished cry, her eyes wide and unseeing. Then she shook herself and came to.

The swollen spot was gone. There was still some evidence of a bruise, but Nichols's forehead was smooth again. He opened his eyes. "What in Circe's tangled loom is going on?"

Remy let out a low whistle. "We'll tell you about it over a cup of tea in the common room. Allan, Masterson, help him up and let's get him back to the house." Then, to Jess, "Will we have to treat him for a concussion?"

"Probably better safe than sorry," she said. "Watch him for the signs and take him to health services if they come up. But he should be clear of severe damage."

Frost got to his feet and offered her a hand up, but Kyle found himself in the way, helping her up with his hands on her shoulders. Frost glared and Kyle found himself glaring back, and he didn't even know why. Frost had probably just saved Nichols's life, if what he was hearing was correct.

"She'll need to eat," Frost said then, but his words sounded spiteful somehow.

"I know that," Kyle said, but inside his own head he was thinking, *really? Is that how it works?*

"Come on. There'll be a midnight feast at the house. If she's with you, it's okay." And with that, Frost walked away, following the others moving off in the direction of Gladius House.

Kyle held Jess for a few long moments in his arms. "Do you want to? Go with them, I mean."

"The Gladius House midnight feast is not something you should miss," Jess said quietly. "But honestly, I really just want to order a pizza and get in bed."

"Okay."

She shook her head. "And I mean get in bed and sleep for a week. I'm sorry, Kyle. I'm just not up to...anything, after that."

Kyle stroked her back. "It's okay. But, hey, do you feel like your arms and legs are made of lead and you can hardly move?"

"Yes," she said. "That's exactly how I feel. But I can make it back to Camella House."

"Okay," he said again, helping her move in that direction, their feet going slowly but his mind racing a mile a minute. That day in poetry analysis class—had he used magic? How else could he explain the seeming miracle of the interpretation just coming to him? And the fatigue afterward? Was that what Master Brandish had been talking about; what hijinks he'd been up to? Had she assumed he'd been doing something wrong with his magic?

He wanted to ask Jess about all of it, but she was even more tired than he'd been. Well, maybe that made sense. All he'd done was analyze a poem. She'd saved someone's life.

"So, Healing Arts, huh?" he said instead.

"Yeah," she said, almost bashfully. "I think I really will declare it. But I've got a few more months before I have to commit."

"That was really amazing."

She chuckled. "*You* are really amazing, Kyle. What are you doing tomorrow afternoon? Maybe I can get Monica to go to the library for a few hours...oh, except that won't work. They closed it for the weekend."

"They did?"

"You didn't read about it? The bulletin should be posted in your common room."

"Oh, um, I guess I didn't notice."

"Yeah, there have been some reports of potential hauntings and they didn't want to take a chance on Halloween weekend with the veil as thin as it is. They still aren't sure if something's going on, or if it's just one of those stories that got out of control."

They were crossing the quadrangle now toward the door of Camella House. "What story?"

"Well, the legend is there's a siren in the stacks, and any student who makes love to her will pass exams. The legend has been around for decades, but lately there's been more talk about it." She yawned widely. "If you ask me, it's just that more students are desperate to spend the night cramming and they go up there and get themselves locked in, and then when they pass their exams, they brag about how they were visited by the siren. It's *always* guys who tell these stories, too. Coincidence?"

"Um, are sirens bisexual?"

"Far as I know."

"Wow, I always thought of them as women who trapped men, but..."

"But that's what you get for listening to mundane versions of myths," she said playfully. "You'll order the pizza?"

"And stay with you to make sure you eat it and don't fall asleep with your face in it," Kyle teased back.

He needn't have worried. Once the pizza arrived, Jess attacked it ravenously, eating six of the eight slices herself while

Kyle finished off the other two. She was deeply asleep when he left as the effects of the warming draught were wearing off and he realized he had no idea where his mask and cape had gotten to. The bell was tolling midnight as he made his way back to the stone edifice he called home.

November

THE COLD weather everyone had been promising arrived. Kyle made Alex take him back to the place where clothes were sold by the pound and they dug through until they found him a heavy, black wool coat—missing some buttons, but Kyle didn't mind that much since it came to only twelve dollars when it was weighed, ten after Alex flirted with the cashier. Jess's roommate Monica, whom Kyle finally met after months of not believing she really existed, sewed buttons on for him, and then he was no longer quite as freezing cold when slogging back and forth to class in the biting wind and rain.

Much to Kyle's annoyance, Jess's heroics Halloween night resulted in her receiving invitations to social things at Gladius House, things Kyle would have rather skipped and spent the time sitting in the suite at Camella 3 West with Jess and the rest of them. But he couldn't very well let his own girlfriend attend "Tea with the Master" at his own house without him. Tea with the Master was a stiff affair, with the men all in jacket and tie, the women either the same or in dresses. Master Brandish and the tutors wore scholars robes and Kyle couldn't help but feel like she was about to bang a gavel and send people to the gallows at any minute. The talk was dull, and they had to sit through Nichols—quite recovered from his Halloween mishap—playing a piece on the cello. The only part that was interesting was when Dean Bell appeared, also in his formal robes, toward the end.

He seemed oblivious to the glare Master Brandish gave him, making the rounds of the student tables, pausing to speak with this one or that. Kyle couldn't help but notice him exchanging a word with Frost. He nudged Jess. "Which one of them do you think is paler?"

She turned from the conversation she had been conducting with Nichols, who had sat on the other side of her after his recital. "Who?"

But Bell had moved on. Kyle noticed Frost fell silent the moment the man moved away. He looked a bit lost without Michael there, which was funny since neither of them ever said very much, other than short remarks to each other. Frost's place in the house was not about to slip because he was getting antisocial, though, not after rescuing a housemate.

Kyle decided to try to get Jess's attention again. "So does Madel—er, Master Finch ever do anything like this?"

"Oh, sometimes. She held a barbecue at her house last spring. She lives off campus by a few blocks. And she'll probably have a Christmas party." Jess declined the tea from the server who appeared. "I bet if she does, you'll definitely be invi—"

They both turned toward the head table as a loud bang echoed through the wood-paneled room. It seemed Master Brandish had gotten to her feet so quickly that she had knocked over her chair.

She and Dean Bell were glaring daggers at each other, then Bell bowed stiffly, turned on his heel, and swept from the room.

Master Brandish turned to right her chair, the sounds of her robe swishing loud in the silence, as no one dared speak. She formed her face into a smile and addressed the group. "Thank you all for joining me. We'll have Christmas tea in a few weeks before you leave for break, as well." Her voice was sickly sweet. Kyle had never heard her like that. "As exams come up, please remember, your tutors' doors are always open, as is mine."

Then she left the room before the impolite murmuring could start.

Kyle took that as his and Jess's cue to escape, too, though he gathered from what snippets he overheard that Bell and Brandish had once been something of an item before he had been made assistant dean. And that no one thought it was all that wise to date someone who specialized in Esoteric Studies, unless you did as well.

Kyle for his part at least now no longer confused Esoteric Studies with Ritual Arts. Somehow in his first week at Veritas he'd gotten them mixed up and it had taken a while of Jess correcting him to get it straightened out in his head. Ritual Arts was all kinds of rituals and power-calling. Esoteric Studies did have a lot of ritual aspects but was pretty much all about sex. She'd finally gotten him to realize "esoteric" was a euphemism— almost a Spoonerism—for "erotic."

"Can I walk you home?" he asked Jess as they crossed the common room.

She kissed him on the cheek. "That's not necessary, Kyle. Besides, you'd need to go get your coat..."

"Okay." He kissed her back, lingering just a little longer than necessary before pulling back.

She nodded to him, then pulled on her mittens and disappeared through the vestibule door.

He knew by now that when they had conversations like that, they were each saying more than they really said. A rough translation of that for someone else would have gone something like this:

Hey, it's not that late, can I come back with you to your dorm and maybe have not-sex with you if your roomie's not there?

No, not tonight, honey.

Well, all right, but I really wish I could.

I know.

It was just as well. Kyle had a major exam in Soothsaying Methods coming up, and he still hadn't memorized all the Tarot cards and their meanings. It was worse than memorizing the periodic table of elements in chemistry class, he thought. But he had to do it.

Maybe he needed help. Someone else to quiz him on the cards, then separate out the ones he got right from the ones he got wrong. He sat down by the fireplace and text-messaged Alex, asking if he could help.

He was surprised by what came back. *No can do, Ace. Up to my eyebrows in this term project myself. Tomorrow, maybe?*

So Alex Kimble *did* study sometimes. That, or he was already engaged in some elaborate goofing off? Kyle stared at the words. Something about them felt like a brush-off. But not like an outright lie.

He went and got his cards anyway, and the accompanying textbook, and returned to the common room looking for someone he could stand. Caitlyn, maybe? Although she mostly acted like freshmen didn't exist in her universe, she might react well to a plea for help.

She was sitting by the window, a book in her hand, but staring at the windowpanes being peppered by more rain. Kyle approached her too cautiously, such that she didn't notice him there at all until he said her name.

"Speyer."

She jumped. "What in Mother Shipton's stinky knickers prompted you to sneak up on me that way?"

"Um, er, I was hoping you might help me with my Tarot studies..." He trailed off as her eyes narrowed.

"Why me?"

Because on Halloween you seemed pretty, and funny, and likable, and even though I was pretty sure you'd treat me like dirt now, I had to try and see if I could be one of the people you'd laugh and joke and fly races with. Or not.

No, he couldn't say that. A lifetime of experience had taught him that people didn't really say what they were thinking, and they got in trouble when they did.

But she was staring at him like if he didn't answer, she was going to casually rip his arm off his body and bludgeon him with it. Or just get up and walk away. *Here goes nothing.*

"Because when we met on Halloween," he said, changing it ever so slightly, "you seemed so likable, and even though I was pretty sure you'd treat me like dirt now, I wanted to see if maybe..."

She laughed. "If maybe I'm not the queen bitch everyone makes me out to be?" Her grin was feral. "It's sweet of you to give me the benefit of the doubt, Wadsworth. Hmm. What kind of help do you need?"

Now, though, people were watching them talk, and he wondered if he could even bring himself to say it aloud in front of everyone. "I'm...memorizing all the cards. I want someone to quiz me on them." There, that wasn't quite like saying, *I'm an idiot and can't seem to memorize them at all.*

"All right, sit down. Nichols!" She called to her classmate, who was crossing the room carrying his cello case. "Come over here."

He obeyed and sat in another chair.

"We're going to help Wadsworth here with his Tarot homework," she said. "You're in Soothsaying, right?"

"Um, yeah. Runes mostly, but yeah." Nichols had shoulder-length brown hair, curled slightly at the ends, and he had a habit of looking down when he talked, his hair swinging down like a curtain and hiding half his face.

"Good."

Kyle looked back and forth between the two of them, a little confused. Did Caitlyn Speyer not know the cards that well, either?

"Draw," she said to Kyle.

He took the cards out of the box and just turned the stack over, then held back a laugh as he saw what card sat there. The Ace of Swords. "Okay, the hero, starting a quest or journey." He set it aside when they both gave him approving nods.

Next card under that was the Three of Coins. "Hard work," Kyle said. "Beginning to see the fruits of labor."

He moved it aside and the hairs on the back of his neck prickled. "Three of...Cups." He swallowed.

"What's wrong?" Caitlyn said with a small frown. "Usually people are happy to see that card."

"I know. It means good luck. Everything's going to work out. It's just..." A coincidence? "I drew these same three cards in this order, once before."

"Well, it was a good reading then, and it's a good reading now, I'd think," she said, "unless the next card you pull has an ominous turn to it?"

Kyle moved aside the Three of Cups and blinked. There were the Lovers. The goose bumps spread across his shoulders. "Wow. Um, well, the meaning on this one is obvious."

Caitlyn patted Nichols on the knee and chuckled. "Are you sure this wasn't all an elaborate set-up to make a move on me, Wadsworth?"

Kyle felt his cheeks go pink. "I already have a girlfriend."

"Ah, right. Torralva. She was here earlier, wasn't she?"

Kyle nodded. Nichols was hiding his face and wasn't even saying anything this time.

"Well, your card reading skills seem to be fine so far," she said, one eyebrow raised skeptically.

Kyle went on through five more cards, naming each one easily, then finally struggling a bit on the Three of Wands. "The wands are tricky," she said, "just like the Scips." She laughed at her own joke on Scipionis House. "They're long and phallic like the swords, but they are deeply magical like the chalices. They're as changeable and movable as fire, so the interpretations can get tricky, too. Although one might say that of any card, given that the context within a reading changes..."

"Don't go over his head, Cait," Nichols warned. "He's just trying to get the single card interpretations down."

"Bah, that's no fun," she said, but relented. "Keep going, Wadsworth. But you owe me a favor."

They went all the way through the deck that way, with Kyle ultimately having to give in and ask for help on more than twenty cards.

"I still say the best way to learn them is not just to go through them over and over, but to give readings," Caitlyn said. "Here, give me the cards. Let me do one for you, Nichols."

Nichols looked up in surprise. "Okay."

She shuffled the cards, then let Nichols cut them. Kyle watched in fascination as she turned up the cards one by one. "Here you are. Hmm, dear me, Nichols, this seems to say you need to be studying a bit harder. Are your grades slipping? No? Something's eroding though in your present. Let's see your future...oooh, you know what this means. You're going to meet your true love! Let's see if the cards will give us a clue when! What's this? A four! Hmm, is that four months or four years, you think?"

And on she went. Kyle was dizzied by how she was able to turn every new card that came up into part of this story she wove around Nichols, each one seeming to corroborate the previous.

She collected them up and handed them back to Kyle. "A lot of interpretation isn't about reading the cards," she said. "It's about reading the person. I get that you have to memorize the basics for your class, but...it's like you're learning to read the alphabet, but you already know how to speak."

She stood up and stretched. "I'll see you two later." She strode away without looking back.

Kyle looked at Nichols. "Are you and she...?"

Nichols shrugged. "Friends with benefits, maybe. I dunno. She's...got her own ideas."

Kyle had a feeling maybe he knew how Nichols felt. "No one really has a lot of time for a relationship here, do they?" he asked, feeling around the issue and wondering if he would be validated.

"Not really," Nichols allowed. "She'd expect to be courted if..."

Kyle could almost hear the unspoken, *if it meant anything to her.*

Kyle wanted to ask if they had sex-sex or only the technical virginity-saving kind. He'd thought for a while that Jess was a rarity, but he was gradually finding out there were others, male and female, who were saving their virginity for magical—not moral—reasons. And maybe that was why there seemed to be a lot of couples who were only a step above friends? Or maybe it was like that in the non-magical world, too, and Kyle just didn't know. *Maybe too many of my expectations have been shaped by bad television.*

They each drifted off into their own thoughts for a while. When Kyle spoke again, he asked, "When's carnival?"

"You mean Carnavale?" Nichols asked in return. "Always the last Tuesday before Lent. Mardi Gras. Same thing."

"Oh, so like, February." Kyle pondered. It would probably be near Valentine's Day, too. He gathered up his things. "Thanks for your help."

"No problem," Nichols said softly, his head tipping toward his lap as he did.

* * * *

"What do you mean, he's not here?" Kyle realized it was a stupid question. Obviously Monica meant what she'd said, that Alex wasn't around. But he supposed it was a human instinct to ask again, just in case the second time the answer might be different.

Monica was a short girl with black-and-red streaks in her hair. Kyle really couldn't guess what the natural color was. She hefted her book bag. "I've got to get to the lab," she said, clearly annoyed at him. "And I'm not Alex Kimble's keeper. Jess ought to be back soon, if you two want to take advantage of the empty room. I won't be back until around dawn."

Kyle sat on the couch and dragged out his cards and books. He'd decided not to worry too much about his final paper for poetry analysis. He'd already written most of it, and it wasn't due for another week anyway, and then they would have a final exam that he wasn't worried about either. Either he'd have a flash of insight on the exam, or he wouldn't. Even if he only barely passed the test, his final grade would be fine. And his poetry writing class was a piece of cake. There was no exam and no final paper. All each student had to do was write a poem a week. His poems lately had been horrible, he felt, but the teacher seemed to like them well enough, and he wasn't being graded against Pulitzer Prize winners either.

Introduction to Alchemy wasn't that difficult either, now that he'd started thinking of it like a science class. He found it a lot like chemistry, and most of the other students in the class had not had any experience at home with doing alchemical experiments or anything, so he felt he wasn't as far behind them. The class was taught in this kind of interesting, folksy way where they recited the charts on the wall, which was interesting to Kyle because that made it almost like learning a strange, avant-garde poem.

But Soothsaying Practices of the Western World left him dizzy and wondering how he could even hope to have a grasp of—or even remember all of—the practices they'd covered. Tea leaves, coffee grounds, molten lead hardened in water, crystal balls, runes, Tarot, flame scrying, palmistry, psychometry, weathercasting—and to think they hadn't even gone into astrology because that was a whole separate class he'd probably have to take later. Most of the class seemed to have grown up taking these things for granted. In particular, he wondered just how much of every day he went around oblivious to omens. He'd known that if you found a penny it was good luck, but he'd thought it was only the ones that were heads up. Apparently, it was all pennies, though. The bit about black cats and walking under ladders, false. But there were other ones his classmates insisted were true and Kyle was finding it harder and harder to keep track of them.

He opened his textbook on omens and tried to read, but was too distracted by worrying to actually absorb what he was looking at.

Thankfully, Jess came in not long after that. "Hello, sweetness," she said, planting a kiss on his lips. "What are you doing just hanging around?"

"Oh, I thought maybe I'd catch Alex to help me with some studying, but apparently he's at the library."

Jess pursed her lips. "I'm starting to think he might really be. At the library, I mean. I've never seen him actually study like this before."

"You don't think he's actually in danger of failing?"

Jess shrugged. "He never talks about it. But it is his junior year. He has to do a pretty major project...maybe he's behind schedule. "

Kyle sighed.

Jess slipped onto the couch next to him. "Want me to help you with your studying instead?"

He put his arm around her and pulled her in for a kiss. "I can think of something I'd rather do. Monica said she's gone to the lab all night."

"Oh? On a Thursday? How funny." Jess's smile turned sly. "But convenient. Maybe you're leading a charmed life, Kyle Wadsworth?"

"Oh, um..."

"I have to write five pages tonight, but come on." She took him by the hand and pulled him into the room. "Maybe we can kill two birds with one stone."

She closed the door behind him. "Take off your clothes and lie down on the bed."

"All right." He put his books down and began getting undressed. "You're not going to?"

Jess put her hands on her hips. "Are you going to argue with me, or do as I say? Trust me, Kyle, you'll like my idea."

"Okay." He stripped down to his socks and lay back on her bed. She leaned over him and tied a strip of soft cloth over his eyes.

The next thing he felt was her lips brushing over his, just enough sensation to make him gasp with surprise before she pulled away. Then her mouth returned, full and wet. He groaned against her tongue, feeling the blood rushing to his groin already.

"So what are you having trouble with?" she asked, settling next to him on the bed. As far as he could feel, she was still fully clothed. She trailed her fingertips down his bare chest.

"Omens and the Tarot," he answered. "Just can't seem to get them fixed in my head."

"All right, then." He felt her breath warm in his ear and it sent more thrills down his skin. "What's the meaning of...the Two of Swords?"

"Um, balance, but it's a precarious balance usually? Like someone may have to choose between two things, but neither choice might be all that good."

"Very good." She pressed a kiss to his temple and he felt her fingertips graze his cock. "Let's say you get five strokes for every one you get right."

He sucked in a breath as her cool fingers took loose hold of his half-hard cock and tugged it gently five times. When she let go, he was nearly fully hard, and her fingers continuing to wander over his nipples and stomach were all it took to bring him to completely straining.

"How about The Moon?"

"Um, wildness. Someone's animal side."

"Rawr. Very good, tiger." She rewarded him with five more soft strokes. "If you keep up like this, I'll have to get the lube soon."

Well, this was certainly a bit different from his previous review session. He tried to imagine doing this with Caitlyn and Nichols then, but found the image to be disturbingly arousing. His cock twitched.

"The Sun?"

"Joy and fulfillment."

"Mm, maybe you get ten strokes for that one, though you're far from fulfillment," she teased. He heard the wet sound of her licking her hand, and had to struggle not to thrust into her strokes.

And so it went, the very gradual build-up of his arousal as she quizzed him on card after card. Eventually she used the lube from the little bottle by the side of her bed, which stayed slick no matter how slowly she went or how long a pause to think he had to take. Sometimes when she liked an answer he gave especially, she would swirl her thumb a few extra seconds around the head.

He was panting and damp from arousal and very close to coming, though not close enough to come on just five light strokes, when she began to quiz him on the omens. Once he'd named off the meanings of a half dozen, she closed her hand firmly around his shaft.

"Your turn to move," she said. "As long as you are naming off omens and their meanings, I'll keep a hold of you. If you falter or have to stop to think, I'll let go."

"Ah! You witch!" he cried, and they both giggled at that, Kyle a little breathlessly.

"I know. I'm a regular Jezebel, aren't I?"

Something in the way she said that made him think he ought to ask her about it...but later. Right now she was loosening her grip. "Rainbows! Rainbow means good luck, and a rainbow over green trees means unconditional love. Acorns falling on you are good luck, too. A grasshopper in the house means..."

What did it mean? Something...

Jess lifted her hand and he made a whine of frustration. "You know it or you wouldn't have said it," she prompted.

"A grasshopper in the house means...a good friend will visit you." She put her hand back, but now he had to keep talking. "Um, a...a cat sneezing is good luck for a bride." He was so close now that as she held tight and he forced his cock up and down through the slick tunnel of her fingers, he was having trouble breathing and speaking at the same time. "Two crows at your window is good luck! Three means a wedding! A flat tire means an inheritance! Falling stars are..." But he cried out as he began to spill through her fingers. Her thumb milked the head as he

came, intense colors swirling in the darkness of his vision behind the blindfold.

He was still panting when she kissed him as if eating the
sweetness of his orgasm on his breath. "I...um..."

She giggled at his lack of coherence and pulled the blindfold
free.

Her smile made him smile. "Hi," he said, like he was seeing
her for the first time that day.

"Hi," she said back.

"I think I'm glad Alex was at the library," he said. Jess kissed
him and wiped his belly with the towel she kept by the bed just
for such messes, carefully wiping her hand as well. He reached
out with one hand to caress her cheek. "What about you?"

"Oh, I have all the things I need to work on my paper right
here."

"No, silly, I mean, it's your turn." He propped himself up on
one elbow to look at her better.

She smiled, but it was her "you're so cute" smile, which normally he liked since he'd usually done something silly to pro-
voke it. But right now, when he earnestly wanted to reciprocate,
it felt a little condescending. "How about you make me come an
extra time this weekend?"

He sagged against her pillow.

She stood up. "You can stay if you want, if you don't bug me
while I'm working."

"No, no, I'll get out of your hair. Once I can move, that is. I
think you turned my legs into jelly."

She laughed. "I'll get you a cola from the fridge."

"Okay."

By the time he was done drinking the can of soda, Jess was
deep in her notes at her desk, typing away at her laptop. She
got up to give him a kiss goodbye, then closed the door behind
him.

He stood for a while in the suite, still basking in the afterglow of what had been one of the strongest orgasms of his life,
but wondering why he felt so out of sorts about Jess. What was
wrong with him? She'd just done something wonderful for him,
not slammed the door on him.

"You okay?"

He looked up to see Lindy standing in her doorway, staring at him. "Jeez. How long have you been there?"

"Couple of minutes. You seem a little out of it." She looked at him. "Do you need a protein bar or something?"

"I just drank something caffeinated."

She shook her head at him sadly. "Jeanie and I just ordered a pizza if you want to share."

"Oh, um, sure."

"Great. Hey, Jean, let's eat out here!"

"Tell me when it's here. I'm going to try to finish reading this chapter first," Jeanie called out.

"Okay." Lindy took a seat on the couch and propped her stocking feet on the coffee table. She patted the seat next to her. Kyle set his book bag down and sat.

"It's a lot to get used to," she said, after the silence had stretched on for a bit.

"What is?" He tried to imagine if Lindy knew what sex with Jess was like.

"Discovering magic. And they used to say they found *me* late. I was thirteen at the time. I guess most prodigies get caught when they're much younger. But eighteen? Jeez."

Kyle had forgotten Lindy was a prodigy. "Thirteen? How did you find out?"

"Oh, I, um...it was kind of embarrassing, actually, but I started setting things on fire."

He felt like he was missing something. "That's embarrassing?"

"Well, when I masturbated."

"Oh."

"Yeah."

They both broke out into laughter after a second.

"A Veritas alumna named Maggie Shipton took me under her wing. It was a bit tricky at first because they had to figure out if my parents could be told the truth or if we had to come up with some kind of other explanation or what. In the end it was decided they'd be told everything, but they're under the same rules we are. Break the silence and it'd mean the Geas. They don't seem to mind, though. For them it's really not that different from having a normal kid go off to Harvard." Her hair was sandy brown and curled over her shoulders, and her bangs were in need of a trim. She folded her hands over her upraised knees. "Mrs. Shipton taught me how to keep the fires from happening, and a lot of other stuff, like the Geas, and make sure you eat after doing a spell...and lots of stuff."

"Did you have a book or anything?" Kyle asked, with some longing in his voice.

"What, you mean like *Young Person's Guide to Magic*? No. Haven't you wondered why you don't have an alchemy textbook? There are a lot of things they don't trust to be written down. And making a book that can't be read by anyone without the Sight? Well, you can make one, like the hand-illuminated tomes in the library, but it would be too much to try to extend the spell to hundreds of copies, and to expect the spell to last for potentially hundreds of years after the person who cast the spell died. So in some disciplines it's oral transmission only, or only by recorded manuscripts in the library. No mass printing."

"I guess Tarot's okay because mundanes know about it already?"

"Yeah. It was already too widespread before magic went underground, and unlike a lot of magical practices that people knew about, it stayed in fashion and wasn't forgotten." She shrugged. "I still feel a little like I need a handbook sometimes, but let's just say I sympathize."

"Thanks."

"It was especially weird right after Jeanie had her accident, but...oh!"

He watched as she jumped to her feet to get her vibrating cell phone out of the front pocket of her jeans.

"Oh yes, be right down! Jeanie, pizza's here! Back in a sec, Kyle." And then she was off down the stairs in her socks.

Jeanie emerged from their room with a stretch. She was wearing pink pajamas and had her hair pulled back in a pink headband. "Hey Kyle, nice to see you. You really need to straighten out what's going on with you and Jess."

"Huh?" He twisted in his seat to see her better. "I mean, I know I do, but..."

"She's got a lot going on in her head and her heart. She can't articulate it all herself, but that doesn't mean it's beyond your power to understand." She sat down on the floor at the coffee table, her legs crossed. "Man, I'm starving. You guys are so lucky you have snacks in your dining hall. It's the only drawback to being in Camella House."

Lindy came back in then, and all three of them began devouring the pizza. Lindy ate two pieces, Kyle two, and Jeanie four. Then Jeanie sat back with a satisfied sigh. "Okay, back to work. You too, Lindykins."

Lindy's sigh was more resigned. "You're right. I need it. See you later, Kyle."

Kyle wondered just when his life would turn around so that he could get more questions answered in a day than he could think up new ones he didn't know the answers to. Jeanie's accident? What did she know about Jess that he didn't? What else could Lindy tell him that maybe no one else could about being magical? What was up with Alex? And why couldn't he live with what a great thing he had with Jess? Why did he want more?

These are the questions that kept him awake that night as he lay on his narrow bed under the eaves, listening to cold November rain hitting the roof above him.

* * * *

The Tuesday before Thanksgiving Kyle went over to Scipionis House for dinner. The crowd was lighter already, as some students who didn't have Wednesday classes had already left for the holiday. He averted his eyes from Frost and Candlin, who were sort of Eskimo-kissing in their seats at a table near the entrance. Normally public displays of affection, even from Frost, didn't faze him, but this one was so sugary, Kyle felt like he needed insulin. They weren't normally so...puppy-doggish.

When he came back into the dining room with a tray laden with food, he saw Frost had gotten to his feet and was putting on his coat and had a suitcase at his side. Of course Frost was going away for the holiday. Almost everyone Kyle knew was, it seemed. Jess was going to an aunt and uncle's house and she hadn't wanted to bring Kyle with her—truthfully, he wasn't sure he was up to meeting scrutinizing family members yet anyway—Lindy and Jeanie were going to Jeanie's parents' house, and Randall even had an invitation to go to some friends of his family's on the Cape and was bringing his roommate, Yoshi, with him. Alex and Monica were the only two from Camella 3 West who would be around, and Gladius House as a whole seemed like it would be empty.

Kyle was just settling into a seat when he saw Alex come into the room. He brightened and was about to wave when he saw Alex say something to Frost, and Frost responding. It didn't look like happy words were being exchanged, though Kyle couldn't hear what they were arguing about.

Suddenly Candlin got to his feet and Kyle felt something like a wave of static electricity go through the air. Candlin spoke through gritted teeth, couldn't have been louder than a whisper, and yet Kyle thought he heard, "Get away from him."

Alex threw up his hands like he wanted nothing to do with them and then walked away, stuffing his hands into his jacket pockets.

Kyle watched him disappear into the food service area. When he looked back, Frost and Candlin were both gone. Then Alex emerged, all smiles.

"Hey, Ace," he said as he slid into the empty chair next to Kyle. "What's shakin'?"

"Nothing much," Kyle said, finally turning his attention to his food. "Had that exam yesterday."

"Yeah? How'd you do?"

"I think I did okay. I didn't walk out feeling like crap, anyway, although I think I got a few things mixed up." He speared a small meatball on his fork and twirled spaghetti around it.

"But graded on a curve, you probably weren't at the bottom," Alex said with a shrug. "You'll live. It'll get easier."

"Will it?" Kyle asked seriously, putting the meatball down untouched. "Like it has for you?"

Alex snorted. "I'm a different case. But by the time you're a junior, you'll be in better shape than I am to pick a junior project. I know you will."

"How can you say that?"

Alex shrugged. "I'm an optimist."

Kyle waited a beat and took a bite of the meatball after all. It was tangy and soft and each bite smelled of basil and oregano. "So what is your junior project? And isn't it for next semester?"

"Well, that's the problem. I'm actually behind by a semester already." He grinned as if to show how ridiculous his predicament was.

"Oh. So you're...if it's not done by Christmas, you're..."

"In really deep doo-doo, yeah." Alex continued to eat as if it didn't matter. "The only one who can give me an extension now is Bell himself, and you know *I'm totally his favorite student ever.*"

"Stop it, you're dripping sarcasm all over me."

"Sorry." But now they were both grinning and Kyle felt a little better. Not about Alex's predicament, but at least it didn't feel like Alex was avoiding him. Of course he wasn't. He really was at the library every night, and no wonder, if he was this close to the wire.

After a few more minutes of their usual banter, Kyle felt comfortable enough to even ask him, "So what was that about with you and Frost ?"

"Oh, nothing much. Just seeing if maybe he could put in a word with Bell on my behalf."

"Why would he do that?"

"Well, I don't think he will, but it doesn't hurt to ask. It's not like I've never done a favor for him." He shrugged. "There is the little matter of the fact that we hate each other's guts, but, well. You never know until you ask, right?"

"You really are something."

"Yup." Alex took a drink from his cup. "So how are you and Jess getting on? I keep thinking I ought to start something up with Monica, you know? Then she'd sleep in my room and you could stay with Jess whenever you wanted."

"Are you serious?"

Alex laughed. "Only a little. Monica and I used to flirt a lot, but...I don't know. She was really overly interested in me while I was with Jess, actually, which was kind of not cool, and if I got together with her, even though Jess and I are ancient history...it would just be awkward all around, you know?"

"I don't, actually. But I can try to imagine," Kyle said. "As for me and Jess...I don't know. Everything we have is great. But I keep feeling like something's missing."

Alex waited for him to go on.

"I always stop just short of saying 'I love you,' you know? Because I don't want her to flip out. I've used the word a few different ways, and we've each expressed a lot of feelings for each other, but...there's something about the...saying it that way..."

"The declaration of love," Alex said with a knowing nod.

"Yeah. The declaration. And she says things that make me think she doesn't want to hear it."

Alex shook his head. "She just doesn't think you're 'the one,' Kyle. You have to do something to show her you are. If you want to be, that is. If she's the one for you, you have to do something to really show her your intention to...to be with her, in a pair-bond sense. I think honestly it's easier—almost unavoidable, in fact—when you're having actual penetrative sex. Don't ask me why, maybe it's just biology, but when you're actually fucking, you can't hold back the declarations, and the wanting to hear them, too. Maybe it's the heightened vulnerability. I don't know. Or maybe it's just that Jess is cold."

But she's not cold, Kyle thought. *She's smoldering hot.* "What do you mean by show her I'm the one?"

"Well, maybe you do need to make that declaration. But not by just blurting it out to her. If she's really the one, have you thought about seriously courting her? Asking her to marry you kind of thing?"

Kyle blinked. "I hadn't thought of that."

"Well? Is she the one?"

Kyle sighed. "I think about her constantly. Sometimes when I haven't seen her for a day or two, I can't eat. It's only through sheer force of will I am not actually living in your suite on the couch just so I can be near her every minute of every day."

"Well, that sounds like you're in love, all right."

"On Halloween, I tried to figure out a way to make her dream come true."

"Her dream?"

"I told you about this, right? About how she had a dream she'd meet her true love at a masked ball?"

"Oh, right. Oh and you thought...yeah, okay, good thinking, Kyle, but I guess what with the broom race going awry like it did, your night didn't go as planned?"

"No." Kyle chewed his thumbnail thinking about it.

"You know…Gladius House used to host a masque."

"Used to?"

"I've seen pictures. Everyone in masks and pseudo-Renaissance finery, a very upper-crust sort of thing, you know, so of course Gladius House was all over it. Very traditional, no one comes with dates, the masks supposedly make you anonymous, or at least give you the thrill of possibly accidentally groping someone other than your intended...but you know, it's all about plausible deniability. She'd know it was you, of course, when you asked her to dance, but she'd see you in a whole new light..."

Kyle could picture it. He could picture it as clearly as if it were happening right in front of him, his hand in a white glove, outstretched toward hers—this would be such a far cry from the senior prom he would have been attending had he not stumbled into Peyntree Hall a few months ago. "How do I make sure this masque happens?"

"Well, your first stop would probably be Brandish's office, unless you want to try to engage the support of some upperclassmen first."

Kyle thought it over. "No, straight to Brandish it is." He'd find out if he really had the knack for saying the right thing then, wouldn't he? "Well, after dessert."

"Sounds good. Get me a piece of that chocolate cake while you're up, will you? Then off on our respective missions we'll go."

* * * *

Kyle went by Master Brandish's apartment, tucked in the back of the first floor of Gladius House. He'd been to her office once before, but never into the apartment, which had an impressive door of some very dark-stained wood, carved in intricate designs. The door knocker was in the shape of a tiger's head, holding the ring in its mouth.

He banged it gently; it sounded quite loud.

The door swung inward, seemingly of its own accord. Kyle had no idea if it was somehow opened with magic, or if it was one of the many things in the magical world that only gave that impression, but if delved into would be revealed to have some other explanation. The door closed behind him and he stared at it a moment, trying to see if there was a visible mechanism of any kind.

"Enter. I'm back here," came Master Brandish's voice from further in. Kyle was in a narrow hall, both walls covered from floor to ceiling with bookshelves, though it was too dim for him to read the titles. He made his way to the end and into the front room, a sitting room that reminded Kyle of the dioramas at historical museums, though he couldn't have quite said what country or what period it represented. Some time when they liked fancy curlicues and gilt edges on things.

The Master was at the small, ornate writing desk, its diminutive size emphasizing her mannish height. "I'll be with you in one moment," she said, as she wrote by hand on a sheaf of paper. "Have a seat."

Kyle sat on a chair that had delicately carved paws for feet. "Tea?"

"Um, no thank you. I just had dinner."

"All right." She capped her pen and placed it in a holder and stood, stretching. She wore what looked like a heavy but comfortable cassock-like robe of brown velvet that covered her from neck to ankle, with matching slippers. She sat on the couch across from Kyle. "A word of advice. If you think the conversation about to ensue might be difficult, say yes to the tea. It will give you something to do with your hands and to cover awkward silences with."

Kyle had never thought of that before. "Um, thank you, but I hope this won't be a difficult conversation at all."

"Oh? What a refreshing change that would be. Usually students only seek me out when they are lonely, heartbroken, about to fail a class, inappropriately attracted to me, or otherwise in dire straits." She laughed lightly. "What can I do for you, Wadsworth?"

"I hear that Gladius House used to host a masked ball. Is there a reason we don't anymore?"

She regarded him. "You're really here on a point of curiosity about house history?"

"Well, yes and no. It was a leading question."

She quirked her eyebrow. "And if I don't have time for leading questions?"

Kyle had the feeling they were fencing with words, and that the Master enjoyed doing so. "Well, my follow-up question would depend on the answer to the leading question." *Touché.*

He was happy to see her smile at that. "Very well. As far as I know, the masques were discontinued around the time you were born for two reasons: fear of AIDS and a general movement at the time, stemming from the department of Esoteric Studies, trying to suppress student sexual activity."

"Oh." Kyle risked one more leading question. "But the department isn't...like that now, is it?"

"We lose talented candidates all of the time because there are initiatory disciplines that can only be performed on or by a virgin. It's a bit of a Catch-22, you see. The students most likely to be uninhibited enough to want to study sex magic tend to be the ones who haven't waited, while the ones who save themselves for moral reasons aren't the ones cut out to use sex as a magical tool." She folded her hands on her knee. "We've been trying to recruit your girlfriend, as I'm sure you're aware."

"Yes. But I guess she's leaning toward Healing Arts," Kyle said, wondering if Master Brandish were going to try to get him to nudge her in that direction.

"We'll know soon enough," she said with a shrug. "Anyway, to your question and the one I think you are about to ask, I do not think there would be objections to us hosting such an event now."

"Wow, yeah, my next question was going to be what you thought about us reviving the tradition, and what would I have to do to make that happen?"

She looked at him for what felt like a long time before answering. Kyle wondered what she was looking for, or what she saw. "Usually an event like that is put on by a committee, four or five students, dividing up the tasks of decoration, publicity, arranging the venue, food, and music. You could probably hold it in Lowell House, like the Halloween ball, easily enough. I can put in the official request. But I'll want to know the names of your committee members before I do."

Kyle blinked. "Wait, does that mean you approve the idea?"

"*If* you can get a committee together. Wadsworth, I don't have to tell you I've been somewhat concerned about your lack of integration into the Gladius fold. I know we don't have many foundlings in the house, both traditionally and in current circumstances, but if Frost can move up the pecking order as swiftly as he has—and with him dating someone out-of-house as well, I might add—then I feel you should be able to."

Kyle tried not to stare. Frost was a foundling, too? Frost, who seemed to know everything about every word wizard? Presumably he was "found" a lot younger than Kyle, though. "I was at the broom race, you know," he said, a little defensively.

"Yes, I do know." She gave him that examining stare again. "Someone needs to become Broomsmaster after Remy graduates, you know. If your aptitude develops along the lines of Applied Enchantment, you might keep that in mind. Replacing the broom Nichols destroyed might take two years, unless Remy's besomic gifts really blossom."

He didn't know what to say to that. "Um, thanks for letting me know."

"You sound skeptical."

"Oh, just, I...haven't even had a class in Applied Enchantment yet."

"Hmm. I'll try to make sure you can register for one. It's easy for us to forget just how behind you are, having come in with no mentor." She moved back to the writing desk and made herself a note. "It might have to wait until next year, but we shall see. Is there anything else, Wadsworth? Anything else on your mind you want to share?"

There were always a million unanswered questions crowding Kyle's brain, but as Master Brandish stared down at him, he found he couldn't think of a single one. "Er, no, I think I've got plenty to think about just now." He stood. "Thank you so much for your time, Master Brandish."

"You're welcome. You may see yourself out."

He bowed and she acknowledged him with a nod, and when he got out in to the hallway, the wooden door shut behind him, the thought in his head was, *She wasn't half as scary as I thought she was going to be.*

* * * *

The next day the campus was half empty, and by dinnertime there was only a handful of magical students left. Only the

Nummus House dining hall opened for dinner, since it was the house with the most students remaining. Kyle still had not been to Nummus House, and he found himself walking there with Kate and Marigold at suppertime. They were going to leave the next morning for one of their parents' houses—he wasn't sure which. And of course, much of the talk centered around who was left.

"Michael's staying, too," Kate said. "It's a shame we won't be here. I feel like we never see him any more now that he's with Frost all the time."

Marigold sniffed. "Just because you don't like Frost..."

"Nobody who isn't a Glad likes Frost," Kate shot back. "Only a Glad would walk around like he's the king of the universe and not get slapped down for it. No offense, Kyle."

"None taken."

"And he's only a sophomore anyway. Tell us the truth, Kyle: where is he on the totem pole in-house? He can't really be that high up, can he? What with spending so much time at our place and everything..."

Kyle thought about it. "He's pretty high up. Yeah, I guess he is higher than all the other sophomores. I hadn't really thought about it before..."

"Hadn't thought about it?" Marigold chuckled. "You really shouldn't be a Glad."

"It's so obvious you should be a Scip. Most of the great poets who weren't Glads were Scips," Kate added.

"No, I think he should have been a Cammy from the start." Marigold poked him gently as they walked.

"So, what's Nummus House like?" Kyle asked, to get the subject off of himself.

"Most of the great Enchanters have come from there," Kate said. "And most of the leading researchers into Tech Magic are Nummies, too."

"Tech Magic?"

"Yeah, like encryption for e-mail that only allows the Sighted to see the text, stuff like that. Their House Master is really fun, too. His name is Karl Zoltan, and he performs magic sometimes in shows and on the street in the Square. Not real magic, of course—which is why his show is so funny. Here we are."

Nummus House was not on one of the main quadrangles of Harvard, but was on a side street, a very large Victorian-era building. Kyle was startled to see a UPS delivery man in brown carrying a package up to the front door. "It's not hidden?"

"Nope. Their old building was, but something happened to it like fifty years ago and they moved here, and there was too much documentation of this building to just erase from everyone's memories. Come on, I'm starving." Kate led the charge up the front steps and through the front door, where a tutor was signing for the package.

The dining room was similar in size and setup to Scipionis House, and Kyle wasn't surprised to see Master Harold Lester was seated at a table with one of the other upperclassmen Kyle recognized but couldn't name on sight. Marjory Ransom, the resident tutor on Jess's hall, was eating with Monica.

Candlin was there, too. Kate made a beeline for him, putting her jacket on the chair next to his, then going to get her food. Kyle followed suit and by the time he got back to the table, Kate was already chatting Michael's ear off about various things. Michael was being his usual quiet self, but he did have a small smile on his face for much of the meal.

Kyle text-messaged Alex, wondering where he was, but he might have eaten something in the Square, or just skipped dinner to spend more time in the library. *I know you're crunched, but tomorrow's a holiday. Let's go roof walking or something tonight.*

The answering text didn't come until much later, past when the library should have been closed. *Can't. All-night research session. Let's have Thanksgiving dinner together tomorrow, though.*

Kyle didn't think anything more about it, and he went back to Scipionis House with the two girls, while Michael begged off joining them. They taught him a card game played with Tarot cards and he lost track of time as they passed the hours.

They had just finished a round when the bell began to ring. The girls exchanged looks. "That's...that's an alarm bell," Marigold said with a frown. The sound of Master Lester's office door banging open made them jump and they watched, amazed, as Lester ran at top speed across the common room and out the door. Kyle gave a glance to the other two and in another moment they were following him. Kyle wasn't sure where they were going but he was even more amazed to see Master Brandish running across the quad as well, a naked sword in her hand. Her path and theirs converged at the Elwyn Library.

Kyle stopped in his tracks when he saw Ms. Finch kneeling on the bottom step, her hair askew and holding a chalice into the air. Brandish ran straight past her into the building. Then Lester reached her, drew a wand from his jacket pocket, and touched the rim of the cup. Fire seemed to leap out in a ring, circling the building. Kate and Marigold stood on either side of him.

"What's the fire for?" Kyle asked.

"It's a barrier, keeps anyone from going in or out," Marigold said in a whisper.

Kyle wondered if Alex were inside the building. "Could this be about the supposed siren?"

"More likely a thief..." Kate said, but she put her hand over her mouth.

Oh, jeez, Alex, have you really put your foot in it this time? Kyle wondered. If Alex had tried to steal a book or something, would he be expelled?

"Oh my God." Marigold pointed.

Dean Bell was emerging from the front doors, carrying someone. From this distance Kyle could easily make out two things, Alex's jacket, and blood. A lot of blood. Bell's hair was loose, and the ends of the long blond strands were matted with blood. Master Brandish emerged a few seconds later, wild-eyed, her sword still in her hand. She pointed the tip at the ground then, taking the hilt in two hands and driving it down into the stone of the top step. A loud cracking sound was heard, then she pulled it free, only to shake her head at whatever it was she saw.

Bell reached the bottom of the stairs just as the man who had to be the Master of Nummus House arrived, much out of breath. He was a dark-haired man with a mustache and ponytail. What was his name? Zoltar or something. Kyle discovered both girls were squeezing his hands tight.

Did magical people pray? Kyle wasn't really sure. He didn't care. *Let him be all right. Please, don't let him die.*

The Nummus House Master knelt at Alex's head the way Kyle had seen Jess do the night Nichols had gotten hurt in the broom race. He placed a coin on Alex's forehead, then his palm over that. The line of fire disappeared, leaving blue spots in Kyle's vision as he tried to see what was happening. The other masters had knelt on either side of Alex's body and had joined hands over him.

Surely if Jess could fix up Nichols, these really powerful magic users will have no problem fixing up Alex. Kyle wasn't even aware he was speaking out loud. "Please be okay, please be okay."

A few minutes passed and no one moved. Finally, Alex did, a kind of spasm. But that was apparently good, as the assembled let go of each other's hands. Ms. Finch got to her feet and came over to them. Behind her, Kyle could see two EMTs were running a gurney down the walkway.

"He's going to live," Ms. Finch said, and her eyes were hollow and her skin drawn.

"Was it...the siren?" Marigold asked in a timorous voice.

"We don't yet know what it was," Ms. Finch said. "But I'd suggest you stay indoors tonight. I've never heard of a siren attacking someone like this—if indeed those rumors are true, and I don't believe that they are. Perhaps Mr. Kimble will be able to tell us more when he regains consciousness."

Master Brandish came over to them then. "I'll walk you back to your houses. Master Finch's advice is sound. You are not to go out of doors until sunrise at least."

They remained silent under her watchful gaze, Kyle just saying a subdued goodbye to the girls at Scipionis House and then accompanying the Master to Gladius House.

"I thought maybe he was going to try to pull an all-nighter," Kyle said. "He's working on some project and really having trouble. So he got himself locked in the library."

"And got more than he bargained for," Brandish said. "Fool."

"Master, if I may ask, what was that you did with sticking the sword into the ground?"

She seemed to become aware of the fact she was still carrying the thing. "Oh, that. Trying a little divination to see where the culprit went. But all it did was point the direction he or she went, which is fairly useless information."

"You think it was a person?"

"It's more likely a person than an actual monster, but as you'll learn if you start on the bestiary, the line between person and monster in the magical world is not very clearly drawn."

"I've been meaning to ask about that..."

"Have you?" The doors of Gladius House were in sight now.

"Yes, um, and I don't mean to be impertinent by the question but...is Dean Bell a vampire?"

Her laughter was immediate and hearty. "Ah, dear Wadsworth. The answer, which I'm sure you're sick of hearing but is nonetheless true, is yes and no. Come and eat something with me quickly and I'll try to explain, if you like."

"Um, all right."

So it was that Kyle learned how to unlock the kitchens—a key on a chain around the Master's neck—and came to be eating cold roast beef on rye on a prep table in the back while Master Brandish explained some things like what a blood mage was and devoured a not inconsiderable amount of food herself. She couldn't linger long, though, heading out to meet back up with the others and continue the search, while deputizing Kyle to spread the word throughout the house that no one was to go out.

As it was, the only other person still in residence was Remy, who was in his room. Kyle could hear the sounds of hammering through the door. Kyle knocked when there seemed to be a lull.

Remy pulled the door open a crack. "Wordsworth?"

"Um, Wadsworth," Kyle said automatically. "Master Brandish said to tell you no one is allowed out of doors tonight."

"Why? Something to do with why the bell was ringing?"

"Yeah. There was an attack, they don't know what did it."

"Attack?"

"A student in the library. Um, very bloody."

Remy's eyes were wide with incredulity. "You saw it?"

"Not the attack, just Dean Bell carrying the student. Master Brandish ran into the library with the sword..."

"You saw the Sword of Gladius?"

"Um, yeah..."

"Wow."

And a cup, a wand, and a coin, Kyle realized. "Anyway, she said don't go anywhere. It might still be dangerous, since the attacker hasn't been caught."

"Okay. Thanks." Remy shut the door.

Kyle climbed the rest of the way up to his own room. First he text-messaged everyone he knew about what had happened. Then he took out his journal and wrote a poem:

When the great invasion storms the shore
Teeth bared, terrible might at the ready
The first to bleed are never the soldiers
Trained to live and die in defense of the land
But the innocent who have the ill luck

To be in the wrong place at the wrong time

"A storm is coming," he said to no one in particular. Then his phone rang. It was Jess. He picked it up and told her what he had seen. It would be far from the last time he'd tell the story that night.

December

IT TOOK Kyle two days of trying before he finally pieced together which hospital Alex was in, since no one would tell
him outright. All he knew was that he was still unconscious. It
took another half day to figure out the best way into the ward
at Mt. Auburn. Alex was in intensive care, and was being kept
separate from the other patients. Kyle wondered if something
went wrong magically, would it mitigate the damage?

That was what he began to think after he had sneaked into
the room, only to be forced to hide behind a curtain almost immediately as two people with familiar voices came striding into
the room mid-argument. Dean Bell and Master Brandish.

"You can't ignore the fact that both of our attempts to track
the culprit have failed," Brandish was saying.

"There is a difference between failure to track and there being nothing to track, Callendra. I have been over every inch of
that library and found nothing. That was true the night before
the attack and that was true the night of the attack as well." Kyle
could hear cloth rustling. Bell was apparently either checking
something on Alex or treating him somehow.

"Are you sure you did the entire building?"

"My dear, wielding the power of the dean's office allows me to speak to the buildings in ways you cannot. I do not believe we have a siren haunting the library."

"And in our midst, Quilian?"

"May not be a siren at all, but something else entirely."

"You are the most infuriating man."

"So you've said."

They went back out of the room. Kyle hurried out, only taking a moment to squeeze Alex's hand, which was clammy and cold. It wouldn't do to get caught there by those two.

* * * *

When Alex didn't regain consciousness after a week, Veritas arranged for him to be transferred to their own facility, Faiella House, a small Victorian house on a side street near the Radcliffe Quad, a bit of a hike from Kyle's room, especially in the rain and sleet that arrived with the month, but still more accessible to Kyle than the hospital had been.

He and Jess went together the first time, and Jess introduced him to a few of her professors, whose offices and laboratories were in the building as well. Alex's room seemed more like a guest room at a bed-and-breakfast than a medical room, but Kyle supposed that made sense. There wasn't anything wrong with him physically now. He'd have some scars across his chest and belly where the creature had gored him, but those wounds seemed to have little to do with why he didn't wake up.

They sat by his bedside, talking to him as if he were awake. But after a while Kyle just couldn't keep it up any more.

He looked at Jess. "You couldn't do for him what you did for Nichols that night? He had a head injury."

Jess squeezed Kyle's hand. "If his problem was a physical one in his head, maybe I could. But it doesn't seem like that. It's more like his mind's in retreat. Gone into hiding."

"Why would a siren attack him?" Kyle had read everything he could about sirens in the past week.

"We don't know it was actually a siren. No one's dared come forward to say they actually spent the night in the library and met the siren, so that might just be a story."

"Then what?"

"Something got loose? Someone's unauthorized familiar?" Jess guessed.

"Did it have to be a creature? Couldn't it have just been a student?"

"Who would attack Alex?"

"Not everyone likes him." Frost. Had Frost already left the campus that night? "Or maybe it was a drug addict or homeless person who had been sleeping there and attacked when they were discovered?"

"They'd have to be magical to get into the building. The library is one of the more heavily secured buildings against accidental incursion." Jess frowned. "There can't have been that many people left. That should narrow the suspects."

"I think Frost was gone already, but there are a couple of Glads who don't seem to like Alex much. Kate and Marigold were with me. Michael was around that night though, and so was Monica..." He looked at her suddenly, an idea forming in his head, but then Alex seemed to stir. "Alex? Are you trying to tell us something about Monica?"

Alex moaned wordlessly, then lapsed into an inert slump again.

Kyle looked back at Jess. "He told me Monica had a thing for him for a while. That she'd been kind of...inappropriate about it and he'd felt weird and told her no."

Jess frowned. "I don't think Monica's a siren."

"Well, how would you know?"

"A siren needs to have sex, for one thing, and she never ever asks me to leave the room for her the way she does for us."

Kyle's leg bobbed impatiently. "But if the campus siren is stalking guys in the library, then she wouldn't need her roommate to vacate the room, would she? And she has all these nights where she's gone until dawn. What would one or two more be? No one would notice..."

Jess's black eyes widened, then she shook her head. "I still don't think so. I would have noticed something by now."

"But they appear completely human except when feeding. And if it was her, and he refused her when she was hungry, she might have attacked him..."

Jess still looked skeptical. "Presumably the reason Alex was in the library was either to study all night, or because he actually hoped to meet the siren, since the legend is that after guys feed it, they pass their exams or whatever..."

"And he was worried he was going to fail! He told me so himself!"

Jess let out a long breath. "You need some evidence that isn't circumstantial."

"Is there a way to prove if someone is a siren or not?" Kyle racked his brains. "Like a blood test or something?"

Now she made a face. "You are not going to convince Dean Bell to test every student here for human-ness. Way too many of us have magical blood from non-human ancestors to want to open that can of worms."

Now Kyle just stared at her. "What do you mean, non-human ancestors?"

"Well, like the siren, for example. They mated with humans all the time back in the days of Homer. Magical biology is not the same as regular biology, Kyle. Alex here has almost certainly got fey roots somewhere back in his family tree."

"And what's Frost? Part naiad or something?"

"What makes you say that?"

"Just, he's so pale, and his hair's so black, and his eyes are so blue, he doesn't look real sometimes." Kyle had no idea what kind of creature he might be, though.

Jess shrugged. "I think he just needs to get out in the sun. Not that that's happening any time soon." She peered at the window, which was showing pitch darkness, even though it was only just past five. "Come on, we better get back."

"All right." Kyle stood and then a new thought occurred to him. "What about Bell himself?"

"What about him? You know he can't actually be part vampire, right? That's just a joke..." She trailed off as Kyle brushed Alex's shaggy hair back off his neck and showed a bruise there, faded and yellow from the intervening week, but still quite visible.

"I overheard him in the hospital say he had been checking the library, and he was definitely hiding something from Master Brandish when they were talking. I could just tell!" he insisted.

"Oh, you are amazing. First you were convinced it was Monica, now you think Dean Bell attacked Alex? Give it a rest, Kyle."

* * * *

After that, Kyle began researching how to detect a siren. After all, if he could prove Monica *wasn't* one, that would make it easier on everyone. And he couldn't really go after the dean, could he? He felt like he had to *do* something. He was registered to take a magical biology class the following semester and had no trouble getting access to those books as "preparation." He should have been studying for his upcoming exams, which were only two weeks away, but every trip to the library produced as much research about sirens as it did on poets and soothsaying and alchemy.

He devoured information, much of which he couldn't really quite digest without learning more, but he eventually did work out a few things. Like that sirens and sphinxes were related, and that there was a kind of charm or amulet that could be made that would make a sphinx tell the truth. If what Kyle read was true, it would work on any "mantic creature," sirens included.

But making it would be no small feat. It required alchemical preparation beyond what he'd done in his class, a ritual aspect he knew nothing about, and had to be completed at the correct phase of the moon. Final exams had to come first. He was going to be staying on campus during the January break; he'd have to come up with a way to make the amulet then.

* * * *

Kyle took to studying by Alex's bedside at Faiella House. He knew Alex's suitemates were making visits but he didn't get the impression any of them stayed long. Everyone was getting stressed over exams. Kyle kept thinking Alex would have been the one to keep everyone loose, make sure everyone had at least a little fun and didn't crack under the pressure, but unfortunately that wouldn't be happening this time around.

"Okay," he said to the unconscious form next to him, the night before his Alchemy exam, "you're really not pulling your weight here, dude. I could use some help with this business about Five Element Theory. How is wood an element? I still don't get that."

Nothing but silence from Alex's quarter, of course.

Kyle closed his notebook. "You're supposed to be helping me with this, you know. Because I could ask Jess, but I'm tired of feeling inferior to her all the time. How am I supposed to get her to see me as 'the one' if she thinks of me as a remedial case? Dammit, Alex, you're supposed to be here." He nudged Alex on the shoulder, speaking softly, but no less frustrated-sounding for his lack of volume. "I don't want to be the only one going into Principles of Applied Enchantment who can't conjure anything. That's your area, right? Enchantment? Come on, Alex, wake up and teach me to conjure. I know it's cheesy, but...come on. Frost does it like it's no more effort than scratching his nose."

Still no answer, but it was like now that Kyle had started talking, he couldn't stop. "What is up with that, anyway? Is that why he looks so washed out all the time, squandering his magic on shit like that? Or was he always such a wan little waif? I swear, that's the only reason he's as high in the pecking order as he is. Showing off his magic whenever he gets a chance.

"Not that I actually give a flying fig about where I am in the Gladius pecking order. But it'd be nice to be able to at least feel like I belong on the same level with Jess and you. Did I tell you I got the go-ahead for this masque thing? Here's the funny part. I had to go and recruit people to be on the committee, right? So I went around and Caitlyn Speyer decided she wanted to make sure it happened, and she ended up recruiting a bunch of other girls, none of whom trusts me not to fuck things up, so... basically I don't have to do anything now. Technically I'm in charge but we've had one committee meeting, I said two words, Caitlyn said the rest, and it's clear they aren't going to let me do anything except be a figurehead.

"Which is kind of good since it frees me up to work on my plan to start courting Jess. If there's one thing the Gladius House library is good for, it's books on manners and customs. I know I can't just...get down on one knee and ask her to marry me. I know I'll just get laughed out of the hall if I try that. But I could give her one of the traditional courting tokens, you know? Show her I'm serious. And serious that I want her to give me a real chance. Oh, what am I saying? It's either going to work or not. She's either going to suddenly realize I'm her dream come true after all, or it's all going to crash and burn worse than the Hindenburg."

He looked up at the darkness outside the window. He needed to go soon. "All right, then, who should I get to show me how to conjure? I sure as hell am not asking Frost. Oh, wait, didn't Marigold say she was good at it? Maybe I'll ask her. Yeah, that's a good idea." He stood up and put his notebook into his bag. "See you tomorrow."

The Scipionis dining hall was quieter than usual when he got there. Between students skipping the meal to study and those there who had books or notes in their hands, and the general atmosphere hanging over the place, Kyle felt almost like he hadn't left Alex's side.

Kate and Marigold came in just as he was toying with his dessert, trying to decide if he really wanted to eat it. He waved to them and they waved back so he was hopeful they'd come sit with him once they were done getting their food.

He wondered about the fact that they were always together. He hadn't really seen anything at all to indicate they were anything but friends and roommates, had he? He tried to remember, but maybe he just hadn't been paying attention. No, he was pretty sure they were just friends.

They did come to sit with him. "It's so quiet in here," he said, as they took seats across the table from each other.

"Is it not like this over at Gladius House?" Kate asked, as she dipped her bread into her soup.

"Well, everyone feels the pressure to do well, but we don't turn the dining room into a library," Kyle said. Gladius's dining hall tended to be pretty sedate, with everyone adhering to manners, but that included not reading at the table and keeping up polite conversation.

Marigold chuckled. "It won't last. As people's exams end, it'll get lively again. Well, except that it will start to empty out as people leave for break. Are you going home for break?"

"No, I got permission to stay here and work on some stuff. I'm still really behind on a lot of things I think I'll need to have down before then." All of which was true, though in Kyle's mind he pictured the amulet he wanted to make.

"Oooh, what are you taking? Do we have any classes together?" Kate asked.

"Well, I got recommended to Master Lester's Poetry and Prophecy class..."

"Awesome! I think I'm actually getting to TA that one!"

"Really? Cool. Then I've got a magical biology seminar. I'm in Principles of Applied Enchantment, and I'm going to take a higher-level poetry writing course."

Marigold took a bite of her salad, then tried to answer, discovered she had too much in her mouth for that, and covered it with a snort. When she could speak again she went on. "I almost signed up for poetry, but Kate convinced me to take Bell's ritual arts seminar with her."

"He's scary!" Kate protested. "I wasn't going to do it alone."

"You wouldn't have been alone, silly. There's twenty people in the class."

"You know what I mean."

Kyle listened to them bicker back and forth good-naturedly for a while. When it got quiet again, though, he put his hands on the table. "So which one of you wants to teach me to conjure?"

They looked back and forth between them. "You can't conjure?" Kate blurted out.

Kyle tried not to look wounded. "I've never tried."

"Really?" They looked at each other again. Kate said, "Wow. The second I heard it was possible I went back to my room and started trying it."

Marigold leaned forward with interest. "I haven't heard this story. What's the first thing you conjured?"

"Money, what else?" Kate grinned. "I was about thirteen at the time. I conjured a five-dollar bill. And I immediately went out and spent it on comic books. Well, after a nap, that is. I never found out if the money disappeared later or what. It wasn't until later I learned that conjured things can fade away again. I hope I didn't get some cashier in big trouble."

"Wow, you just got a five-dollar bill like that? I had to start with pennies and work my way up. And I had to start with one in my hand and make more of it. That is so much easier." She gave Kyle a sly look, then took a five-grain roll off Kate's tray, held it in her hand, said "Presto!" and there were two.

"Hey, make sure you give me back the real one!"

"Silly. I'm sure I did it right. If you eat it before it disappears you should be fine." She handed one back, then turned to Kyle. "That one works best with bread and with fish, for some reason."

"Because fish are less evolutionarily evolved than mammals," Kate said.

"Evolutionarily evolved?" Marigold said with a snigger.

"You know what I mean."

Kyle got up and came back with a slice of bread. He held it in his hand. "Okay, so what do I do?"

Marigold frowned slightly, a crease between her eyebrows. "Do you have an exam tomorrow? Because the first time can sometimes really wipe you out..."

"Oh. Um, yeah. Poetry Analysis," Kyle said. "It's an essay one, too, so I kind of have to be awake for it."

"Then you really ought to wait."

"Okay, I'll wait. But what do I do?"

The two of them shared another look. This time Kate spoke. "You just kind of...make it happen."

"Yeah," Marigold agreed.

"I don't have to say anything, or wave it around or what have you?"

Kate took a bite of her roll. "Well, you could. You could increase the power of the spell with a preparatory ritual, and maybe enhance the effect with alchemical boosting, and you might find a word of power that helps you tap your own energy. There are lots and lots of ways to gather your power. But the basic action is still the same. You still have to just...do it."

Marigold sighed and got up from the table. When she came back, she had packed a bunch of things in a to-go box the staff had put out for the students who were taking their meals with them to their labs or to study more. "Here. Take this. Because I *know* the second you get back to your room, you're going to try it. Just make sure you've set your alarm first, so you're not late for your exam."

"Oh, it's not until two in the afternoon," Kyle said.

Marigold gave him a look. "Like I said. Make sure you've set your alarm first."

* * * *

Kyle went back to his room with the box of food and a head full of thoughts. After staring at the penny in the palm of his hand for a long time, then switching it to the other side and trying again until his eyes began to hurt because he wasn't blinking, he gave up and wrote a poem.

Alchemists saw in ancient times
Lead and gold are nearly twins
But the secret they could not divine
Was in the heart, not in the mind
There is a lock deep inside
And a key too small to be seen
But lead to gold I will provide
And like to love, your heart will glean.

He crossed out "provide" and "glean" ten times over and wrote them in again each time as he failed to find better substitutions.

Teen love poetry is always awful, he reminded himself. *Just get it out of your system and forget it.*

But he didn't forget it. The next day, during the poetry analysis exam he kept coming back to it in his head. This idea of the alchemy of emotions, and there being a fine line between like and love, and loving as friends and loving as something more. And the fact that he couldn't seem to achieve either transformation just with the power of his will.

He was pretty sure his essays came out okay even though his mind was only half on them, and he was still in a bit of a fog, thinking about the poem and the ideas he was trying to untangle with it, when he nearly ran into Jess on the steps of Robinson Hall.

"Jess, what are you doing here?"

"I figured I'd meet you and we could go grab dinner together," she said.

"Sure." They began walking toward Scipionis House.

"Actually," she began, after they had gone a few steps, "I was thinking maybe we ought to treat ourselves to dinner out somewhere."

"Oh?" He knew that meant a date. With Jess, "dinner out" always meant "dessert," too. "Is Monica gone already?"

"She's actually staying through the break, but she's out to-night," Jess said, but her voice was more somber and serious than he would have expected for such an announcement, but he understood when she went on. "Kyle...I...I've decided to leave tomorrow instead of waiting until Sunday."

"Oh." He was staying through the holiday, but she was go-ing home. "Tomorrow is...tomorrow. Soon, I mean."

"I know. I'm sorry. My aunt Maria's only coming for a few days, and my mother needs help getting ready for everyone, and...I changed my ticket already." She bit her lip. "Are you mad?"

Kyle stopped in his tracks. He put his hands on her shoul-ders gently. "I'm not angry."

"But you're upset."

"Well, a little. I'm going to be counting the days until you come back as it is."

Her expression softened. "I know." She pulled him close, still looking at him. "It's just your luck they changed the schedule, too. The break's longer now."

"I know. I've been hearing no end of whining from the Scips about how they liked having the whole break to study for ex-ams," he said, mustering a small smile. "Personally, I'm glad to get them over with. So where do you want to go?"

"I know I'm going to be eating Spanish food for the next month at home, but...we haven't been back to that place since our first date." Her smile made her face glow a little, and Kyle's heart skipped a beat.

"Okay. You order, though."

"Of course." She held his hand all the way to the restaurant and Kyle decided that the feeling of being in love itself, irre-spective of reason or direction, was cause for celebration. No wonder there were so many poems about it.

* * * *

By the time they got back to Jess's room, Kyle's head was spinning. Jess had made friends with the owner and the next thing he knew, they were being treated to some sangria. Kyle had never had wine, and this was wine and fruit and who knew what else, and it was very hard to drink it slowly. Jess didn't seem that affected. She said her family drank wine at home all the time. She'd been allowed to have a tiny glass of it, watered down, since she was about ten, and regular strength in small amounts since she was a teenager.

Or maybe she *was* affected. She hung on his arm as they walked across the campus, and although she was always affectionate, she seemed even more so. Or maybe that was how the wine affected Kyle. Everything seemed softer and more touchable and warmer.

She lit candles all around the room, filling the air with some exotic flower's scent, and turned on some music with a sinuous sound, violins and sitars and drums. Then he found himself sitting on the bed, watching her undress to the music, peeling her clothes off layer by layer in the most enticing manner she could, looking up at him with her dark penetrating stare, then glancing coquettishly away.

When she was wearing nothing but her earrings and a bracelet, she pushed him back on the bed and started undressing him with great glee, like he was a gift on Christmas morning. She seemed delighted to find his nipples, bending down to lick and suck them, then even more so to discover his cock, already almost completely hard in anticipation.

She crawled over him, pressing a kiss to his mouth, then turning around to put his head between her knees and take his length into her mouth.

This was something new, but the scent of her mixing with the orchid or jasmine or whatever the candle aroma was made his mouth water, and he fitted his hands in the small of her back, pulling her down so his tongue could reach her clit. He'd licked her to orgasm before, but never while she was sucking him at the same time. He suckled at the sensitive nub, flicking it with his tongue and making her jump, then switching to long, soft strokes.

He lost himself in the vertigo of wine and music and scent and her body, the light flickering like a movie seen in a dream. Every time he opened his eyes, her skin looked made of bronze, the globes of her ass perfect and unblemished. Time ceased to pass, until at some point he decided it would be better if she came first. Jess could come two or three times as often as he could; if he spilled now it'd be a half hour before he could go again. He began making a more concerted effort to push her arousal higher, flicking his tongue more directly where it counted, then slipping one finger into her to tickle her G-spot the way she'd taught him to.

She came almost instantly when he did that, the vibrations from her moans going straight through his cock, as she kept it in her mouth. She finally pulled it free when her orgasm had subsided and she caught her breath. She turned around then, placing kisses up his torso until she reached his mouth, still slick with her juices.

"I want to do something special for you," she said softly, "since it's the last time you'll see me for a while. I'm really going to miss you, you know. What would you like?"

He looked up at her, tendrils of her hair curling down toward him. "I like everything, you know that," he said with a chuckle.

"But don't you have a favorite thing? Of all the things we do? Or something new you want to try?"

His cock throbbed and he swallowed hard. "The only new thing I want to try is something we said we wouldn't," he said, his voice hoarse with suppressed emotion. He had a strong suspicion that when he did try it, it would quickly become his "favorite" thing. "Although there are probably things to try I don't even know about."

She grinned at him. "Are you so tempted that I shouldn't even let you come between my legs?"

"Oh fuck, Jess..." He shuddered as she reached down and stroked his cock. "It's...it gets harder and harder not to."

"I know," she whispered. "I know."

The next thing he knew, she was straddling his legs and rubbing her clit and slippery lips up and down his cock. He groaned and gripped her bedcovers tight, to keep himself from reaching down to her hips and trying to get inside her.

She shuddered, moving her hips faster, jerking them. "Mm. Think...think I'm going to come, rubbing on your cock like this..." And suddenly she cried out, rubbing not just there, but her cheek against his cheek, her breasts against his chest, a sudden frenzy of friction as she came again. "Oh, Kyle..."

Now he did slip his hands around her back, over her buttocks, to the back of her thighs. "I want to come with you rubbing me, then," he said. "Just like you are."

"Mmmm. I might have another one before you get there, unless you're close..."

"Please do," he said with a feral grin. "The more, the merrier."

She began to move again, but this time he urged her into a rhythm that suited him just a little better. Again he sank into sensation and music and scent, losing himself, but never so much that he forgot the rules. When orgasm seized her again, he crushed her tight against him and thrust up against her, pushing her toward his feet a little so that now, as he snapped his hips upward in that desperate last kick for the finish line, the head of his cock slid along her stomach. A burst of hot wetness made the way suddenly slicker as he came, and he kept her tight against him as he milked more spurts out with more thrusts.

He wasn't aware of having fallen asleep or blacking out until he felt a cool cloth on his forehead, and then her lips kissing gently across his brow.

"Wow," he said.

"I am really, really going to miss you," she said again, as she tossed the cloth aside and snuggled down next to him.

"Yeah," Kyle said, wondering how long he had been out. Long enough for her to clean him up and pull up the blanket, anyway. "I don't know how I'm going to get through it. I've never...had anyone I was going to miss this much."

"No one?"

He thought about that a moment. "I never knew my parents, so I never missed them. There was, well, there was Jove, I guess."

"You haven't mentioned that name before," she said, as she rested her arm across his chest.

"He was a cousin of mine, but a much older cousin, like...I'm not even sure how old he was. In his twenties, I guess, when I was ten, eleven, twelve...He came to live with me and my great-aunt for like two years. The two of them fought all the time. It

wasn't a very good situation for him. He up and left suddenly..."
He broke off speaking and shrugged.

Jess lifted her head. "You've got tears in your eyes."

It was such an old hurt, Kyle didn't even realize he could
still feel it, until now. "He never even said goodbye. Just...ran
off. I kept...I kept thinking he would show up again, or he'd
write me or send a postcard from wherever he was..." He drew
a long slow breath, trying to keep the tears from falling.

"It's okay," Jess said gently, planting a line of soft kisses
along his jaw. "Sex makes you vulnerable, you know. It opens
your heart in all ways."

He swallowed. "I don't want to cry over someone I don't
care about anymore," he said, letting the breath out as slowly as
he'd taken it in.

"Okay," she said, and kissed his eyelids, one and the other. A
few stray tears wet his lashes. "I promise I'll be back."

"Okay," he said, and let her kiss him and stroke his hair softly until he fell asleep.

* * * *

Christmas morning, he went to visit Alex. He hung a small
stocking on the window sill for him and told him he'd have to
wake up to get what was in it, and who on Earth could sleep on
Christmas morning anyway? But Alex didn't stir.

"Well, it was worth a try, I guess." Kyle sat down next to him.
"You missed how it started snowing last night when I was on
my way back from dinner at Ms. Finch's. Yeah, she took pity on
me, seeing as I'm one of the only ones actually staying around.
It was the weirdest dinner ever. Her and me, and the first-floor
tutor—what's his name, Hansen? I can't remember why he's
staying—and her next-door neighbor, and Professor Bengle,
and Master Lester and his daughter and her husband whose
names I've forgotten."

He kicked off his boots and leaned back in the chair, putting his feet on Alex's bed. "It was great food. I'd never had
goose before, and after the meal Ms. Finch brought out these
things called crackers. You probably know all about this, but
we pulled them and they sort of exploded, and everyone got a

hat to wear, a horrible pun to read, a piece of candy, and a toy. I could use your help with the toy."

There was no answer. Kyle dug it out of his pocket. "It's a puzzle, you see, with these little pieces that were supposed to be difficult to get apart. Well, I got it apart in just a few seconds, to which Master Lester said then of course, for me the puzzle is how to put them back together. Obviously they must go together because that's how they were, but I'll be damned if I can figure it out now."

He fiddled with the pieces in silence for a while, but he didn't get anywhere with the puzzle and eventually started talking again. "So what's up with your family, anyway? Why aren't any of them here visiting you? Do you really have fey blood? That makes you...part elf, does it? I'm probably getting that wrong. I got into a magical biology class for next term, so maybe I'll know more about that kind of thing in a few months.

"I've been reading a lot about sirens, though. It's confusing stuff. I mean, if there's an actual siren-siren around, it's one thing. Very hard to catch, I know. But if it's a student or a person who just has a lot of sirenic bloodline, it complicates the issue, doesn't it? Well, I've got a lot of time on my hands. The catch-up reading they have me doing during break...I can't really do it more than two or three hours a day. So the rest of the time, I'm working on these two projects. One, to make this amulet that will tell if someone has mantic blood. I'm not totally sure what mantic blood is, except that it applies to sirens and to sphinxes. Supposedly it'll make the siren answer my questions, anyway.

"The other one, of course, is Project Jess, and man, it would really be so much easier if I could conjure. Or even transmute. There's a graduate tutor in the house who did a whole thing for her master's degree where she made a pumpkin into a carriage, mice into footmen, the whole nine yards from Cinderella. It was like twenty things all total, something crazy like that! Then at midnight, bam, it all changed back, and she said she slept for a week afterward. But man, that sounds cool, doesn't it? I know, it took her years to perfect all the steps, and a whole year just to muster up the energy to focus into it all at once, but...yeah. I was impressed. Unfortunately, she's gone for the break, just like everyone else, it seems.

"Well, okay, not everyone. Monica is still around, but hardly anyone I know. They closed the dining halls except for Nummus again, because there are only like twenty of us or something. At least they're letting us stay in our rooms. And Nummus is sort of on the way here..."

He sighed as he ran out of things to say. He stayed for a little while longer, holding Alex's hand, but there was no reaction. "Well, when you wake up, your stocking's on the window sill. Merry Christmas, Alex."

January

THE PRISTINE beauty of the first snow had faded by New Year's Eve as rain and sleet and more snow piled on, and Kyle didn't see the sun for a week. He would be spending New Year's Eve at Scipionis House, where a couple of the diehard graduate students had declared a party. Kyle was curious what a party run by Scips would be like, picturing a bunch of people gathered around a Scrabble board.

When he arrived, he was surprised how many people were there. He was by far the youngest, one of the only undergraduates he could see. Where had all these people come from? Then it dawned on him that there were grad students who lived off campus, who weren't counted in the two dozen or so staying through the semester break.

Lively music played from a portable stereo set up on the mantelpiece and people were bopping near it without quite fully committing to dancing. Nearly everyone he could see had a paper cup or a mug in their hand.

He wished either Jess or Alex were there. Alex would have fit right in. No one was dressed up, most in jeans and flannel shirts. Even Master Lester was dressed down, having swapped his tweed jacket and elbow patches for a comfy-looking cardigan sweater. Well, that was someone he could talk to.

"Happy New Year, Master," he said, approaching the old man with a smile.

"Ah, and Happy New Year to you, Kyle. I understand you'll be in my class on Interpreting Prophecy this term?" Master Lester grinned at him, as if very pleased by this notion.

"Yes, looks like it," Kyle said. "I just hope I can keep up."

"Oh, I'm sure Katalethea will help you out. She thinks very highly of you, Kyle."

He must mean Kate. "That would be nice. Everyone else seems to have a background of common knowledge and stories that I don't."

Master Lester's grin dimmed for a moment while he considered this. "Ms. Finch had mentioned something about you staying on during the break for make-up work, but she didn't say in what. Would you like a head start on some of the texts? You can't remove them from this building or the library, but you can read them and take notes, and there are commentaries, oh, there are commentaries! Some of them quite unreadable but others are a delight. You may want to start your own."

"My own commentary?"

"Yes. A diary, in a sense, of you writing about the prophecies you read, recording your interpretations, and having a conversation, if you will, with the author." He beckoned Kyle to follow him to the door of his office and then bade him stand there while he rummaged in his desk drawers. "Here we are."

Lester brought out a leather-bound book and handed it to Kyle, who reflexively flipped through the pages to find them all blank.

"A belated Christmas gift, if you like. Though once the pages are full, it'll be your gift to your future housemates. I'm sure the Gladius House library is as full of alumni commentaries as our own is."

Kyle ran his hands over the rich leather of the cover, textured and soft. "Oh, but...I see. Thank you. Thank you very much."

Lester chuckled. "As usual, my timing is off, though. Now you'll have to carry it around all night. Hmm, perhaps you'd better put your name in it." He gestured to the desktop where there was a cup full of pens.

Kyle put the book down and lifted a pen with caution, then wrote his name with care on the front page. No blood, no sharp pain.

Master Lester watched him curiously, but said nothing about Kyle's odd behavior.

Back at the party, Kyle found he didn't want to let go of the book, so he carried it in one hand, a drink in the other, drifting from conversation to conversation. He had to put it down, though, when he made his way over to Marjory Ransom, the only other person there he knew somewhat. Her eyes lit up as she saw him and held up an orange in her hand. "Kyle. How lucky."

"Lucky?" he asked, looking more closely at the thing she was holding out toward him. It was an orange, but the rind was studded with cloves.

She smiled. "It's a clove orange."

"I can see that. But what does it mean?"

"Well, if someone offers you a clove orange, you're supposed to either say 'no, thanks' or you take a clove out with your teeth, and you kiss the person you got the orange from." She placed the orange in his hand.

It smelled lovely, the scent of clove and orange peel seeming to evoke a memory—except he'd never smelled it before. Marjory was smiling up at him, smug and sweet. She had cat's eye glasses, and dark brown hair pulled straight back from her face in a ponytail. "And I don't have to do anything magical for it?" he asked.

Her eyebrow quirked upward. "Who says a kiss can't be magical?"

He blushed, recalling she was doing graduate work in sex magic. "And Jess won't be angry with me?"

"I'm sure if she were here, she'd play, too. The clove orange is just a very slow, ongoing party game. And everyone wins."

"All right." He kept his eyes on hers as he drew a clove out with his teeth. He held it there, trying to decide what to do next. He hadn't exactly kissed many girls, and none in a room full of people, but he put a hand on her shoulder to draw her close, thinking, *a kiss can be magical...*

Marjory's lips were soft and almost tentative, and felt so different from Jess's that Kyle almost pulled back, startled. But he applied just a bit more pressure and her lips parted, as she yielded to him in a way he had also never felt before.

When he pulled back, he was short of breath and Marjory was beaming. "Thanks, Kyle!" She grinned and walked away from him with a little wave.

He sat down on the edge of the hearth to catch his breath, and then it dawned on him he had the orange and had to find someone else to pass it on to. Could he just give it back to her? She hadn't said there was a rule against kissing the same person twice, but—

But that really began to feel like cheating on Jess. Because now he wanted to kiss Marjory again, to see if the second time would be like the first, or if the effect would have worn off some. He took the clove out of his mouth and tossed it into the flames.

It was probably best to find someone to give the orange to sooner rather than later. He looked around for a likely candidate. There weren't many girls standing alone. Perhaps if he wandered around some.

He took a walk out of the common room toward the dining room, hoping to find someone nice-looking browsing the bookshelves in the hall or on her way to or from the ladies' room. He came to another room he hadn't seen before, a smaller library. A group of five students had circled the chairs and were passing a bottle of something around the circle.

"Wadsworth, isn't it?" said the blond woman holding the bottle.

"Um, yes," he said, coming into the room properly from the doorway. He couldn't quite place where he knew her from, only that she looked familiar.

"If you'd like a bit of this, I'd suggest you sit," she said, prompting chuckles from the others. She patted the empty chair next to her.

"I, um, should probably get rid of this, then?" he said, holding up the orange.

"Ah, yes. That should make it interesting." She patted the chair again.

As he sat he remembered her name. Kendrick. Polly? Patty? Something like that. She helped to run the Alchemy lab sometimes and graded their midterm exams.

Kyle handed her the orange. A moment later, she pulled him into a deep kiss, and her tongue tasted of something spicy beyond the clove in her mouth. When she let him go, she handed him the bottle, indicating it should go from him to the fellow on Kyle's left, while she turned to hand the orange to the girl next to her. Kyle tried not to stare while the blond woman and the African-American woman kissed, but he'd never seen two women kiss before, other than publicity stunt kisses on TV. He turned to the man beside him.

The guy had wire-rimmed glasses and a neatly trimmed beard. "Just lift it to your nose and sniff," he said, miming it with his hand.

Kyle nodded, then took a sniff of the potion.

A moment later he wondered why he was lying on a rolled-up newspaper. Then the world righted itself and he realized it was actually someone's arm behind his back, and that they were helping keep him upright.

"Has quite a kick, doesn't it?" The guy said, taking the bottle carefully from Kyle's fingers and then sniffing it for himself before passing it on.

Kyle found his tongue had forgotten how to cooperate with his lips to form words. He nodded instead. He wanted to ask what the stuff was called, but just breathing was taking up most of his attention and focus.

Thus he was surprised when the man held up the orange. Oh. Right. It had gone around the circle the other way. Kyle swallowed hard. "Oh. Um."

"Wow, I've never actually seen the deer-in-the-headlights look before," Kendrick said with a laugh.

"You can say no...?" the man reminded him with a raised eyebrow.

But by then, Kyle's alchemy-numbed brain had decided that if he didn't go through with it, it'd be disgraceful somehow. He took the orange, took the clove in his teeth, and leaned in.

The beard was tickly, and the hand that slipped behind his neck felt disconcertingly strong, and he completely lost the clove in the small battle of tongues that ensued. Then he was free, breathing and blinking hard. "Um, thanks," he said, just to prove he could speak again.

"You're quite welcome."

He handed the orange to Kendrick, who kissed him even harder, then got to his feet. "Um, thank you, everyone, but I just remembered I left a book in the other room and I shouldn't lose it." The buzzing in his brain that had started with the bottle was still going on, so he felt a bit weightless as he took a step, and like their voices saying goodbye were already far away.

It wasn't until he was lying in bed that night, still feeling a bit like gravity had not quite returned, that he realized he'd never learned the guy's name.

* * * *

The next week went by slowly, so slowly, with nothing to do but study commentaries on prophecies and eat and work on creating the amulet. He ended up buying a chain with an arty medallion on it to use for the spell, off the clearance rack of one of the clothing stores in the Square. He had pretty much all the ingredients he needed. There were a few preparatory steps, and he fretted over whether he really needed a wand or not—the opinions of the experts were split on that issue. Then it was back to the prophecies again.

The Avestan Prophecy, First Cycle in particular drew his attention. He remembered that poem of Eliot's. Surely Eliot had read the prophecy himself during his time at Veritas.

What house had he been in? Kyle went to Master Lester the night before the new moon to ask.

"Eliot? I'm honestly not sure," the Master said, sucking on his empty, unlit pipe. "I would assume yours, if I don't find him in the Scipionis House rolls. Hm. Let me look..." He dug into a file cabinet and brought out a ledger that he pored over for several minutes. "Hmm, no, not here. Ask Master Brandish, my boy."

And as Kyle had been turning to leave, he'd added, "Longfellow was a Glad, you know."

Master Brandish was not in when he sought her, so he perused the books in the common room. Many of them were diaries of the house's past residents. Could there be—?

No Eliot, but Kyle found his fingers shaking a little to pull out a slim volume, lettered on the side: "Lngflw."

He opened it to find a book of poems, interspersed with notes. Notes! And the poems had some corrections and changes made by hand.

He opened to a passage:

I stood on the bridge at midnight,
As the clocks were striking the hour,
And the moon rose o'er the city,
Behind the dark church-tower.

I saw her bright reflection
In the waters under me,
Like a golden goblet falling
And sinking into the sea.

The hair on the back of his neck stood on end. Who was *she*? He couldn't help but see her as the same woman in Eliot's poem. But where Eliot's poem was in the evening, now it was midnight, and she was irrevocably lost?

He took the book with him up to his room, but couldn't shake the feeling of melancholy that had come over him. He put the books and prophecy notes away and tried again to turn the penny into two pennies, or a nickel, or anything other than what it was.

Nothing. He gave up and put it back in the pile of loose change on his desk. He ended up lying in bed listening to music and staring at the ceiling, his mind blank.

He wasn't aware of falling asleep until while he was sitting on Jess's bed talking with her, she said, "You know this is a dream, right?"

"Damn, is it?" He sighed. "Wait, but are you really talking to me through the dream? Are you dreaming this, too?"

"Does it matter?" she answered, her eyebrow cocked so Jess-like it felt like it had to be real and not merely a dream.

He grinned. "Well, I hope neither of us dreams that Monica walks in."

She laughed. "As long as she's not dreaming, too, we're safe." And she pulled him down into a kiss.

Her mouth was wet and soft, and his hands searched for her skin under her clothes. It was a dream, which made him wonder if he could just wish their clothes away.

She gasped as his cock grazed her bare belly. Apparently so. He rutted against her a few times, suckling at her neck where she liked it best. Then he gasped as he took hold of his cock in her fingers, stroking him. "So if...if this is a dream...does it count?"

"What do you mean?" she asked, licking his chest and tugging on his cock with the ring of her fingers.

"I mean...can you lose your virginity in a dream? Or not?" His cock was throbbing as he imagined what he was speaking of.

"Oh." Her eyes lit up, and his cock twitched in her hand. "No, technically until an actual penis penetrates me down there, I'm fine."

"Jess," he breathed. "Jess...Do you want to?"

But suddenly he was awake. Had a noise woken him? What time was it? He sat up to check his phone and hissed, his erection painful in his shorts. Nearly three in the morning. And the phone had not rang, no messages. He text-messaged her to see if she was awake, but got no answer.

He wrapped his own hand around his shaft and hissed again, as the skin felt feverishly hot. He lay back down to take care of business, trying to sink back into the dream, imagining it was her hand and not his pulling him briskly toward orgasm, but his mind would not stay on the images he tried to steer it toward, wandering through thoughts and suspicions and speculations and poems.

Tomorrow was the new moon. Tomorrow he would try the spell to create the amulet that could make a Sphinx tell the truth.

And if I'm not magical after all? Kyle could see his future disappearing like the cup sinking in Longfellow's poem about the bridge. No. No, that wasn't going to happen. He had to keep his confidence up. He knew that much by now, that self-doubt was the worst of the self-fulfilling prophecies someone could inflict on themselves; it could doom a spell to failure.

But he hadn't managed a single conjuration or transformation yet, couldn't levitate things, couldn't talk to animals—and had felt stupid trying—and had yet to have any prophetic visions of his own.

Coherent thought ceased as he drew closer and closer to his peak, the sound of his own breathing loud in his ears. He rolled over onto his stomach, licking his palm and pushing it under himself so that he could rut against it. He buried his face in his pillow to muffle the noises he was making—not that anyone was around to hear, but he did it out of habit. His hips jerked as he broke into a sweat. So close, he just needed a little more...

He threw his head back violently as he came, the orgasm sending a spasm through his whole body. His shoulder knocked painfully against the corner of his desk, which was crammed next to the bed in the tiny room, but he just gritted his teeth and rode out the waves of pleasure that rocked through him.

He shook his head as the sound of something metallic reached his ears through his post-orgasmic haze. He looked. Loose change was spilling off the desk onto the floor.

Wait. That was definitely more change than was there before, wasn't it?

He looked over the edge of the bed at the floor. That looked like a dollar or two worth, and there was at least that much on the desk.

He hurried to clean himself up and then set to counting it. *I have no idea how much there was to start with,* he thought. But it definitely seemed like more. Maybe twice as much as had been there?

He decided to believe that it was. Yes, that was it. Believe that he'd done it, yes, and now wasn't he starving? Surely that was proof?

Good enough. He got dressed and put on his coat and gloves for a walk to the all-night drugstore to get a protein bar. The tiniest sliver of moon was visible over the roof of Widener Library as he crossed the yard. *Who wrote or will write the poem that described the wee hours?* he wondered.

When he got back to his room, laden with protein bars and chocolate-covered peanuts and a handful of other things he'd only been half aware of buying, he wrote:

A shred of mist clouds God's eye
Nearly closed, the last sliver of moon

Dragged into sleep by the weight of waiting dreams
While hopes escape like precious breaths lost

* * * *

In the morning he woke to find he'd written the poem in Longfellow's notebook, not the one Master Lester had given him. He stared at the page in a panic for a moment, then a kind of calm descended on him as he realized there was no undoing what he'd done. He had to accept it.

Very well. He added a notation that included his own name, the date, a description of walking toward Widener, and his persistent thoughts about the Avestan Prophecies, "in particular the first and most famous cycle."

He slipped the book back onto the shelf on his way to breakfast, but after walking ten or so steps past the door, heading toward the Nummus dining hall, he suddenly wondered if he should fast before the ritual tonight.

Maybe I should jerk off, too. The moment he thought of it, he knew he would. He blinked, wondering if this was what prophetic moments felt like. It all seemed so clear somehow.

What he should have done, he would later think, was go to dinner and box up some food to eat later, but after not eating all day, he was afraid he would be too tempted by the dining hall, and would give in and eat something.

Instead, he just stayed in his room that day, preparing the ingredients and memorizing the words to the ritual. They were in Greek, since it was the ancient Greeks who had perfected this technique. He didn't know if translation would really work, so it was probably best to just go with what was proven. He was sure his pronunciation was atrocious, but everything he'd read so far said that wouldn't really matter.

He had checked the astronomical charts, and it seemed to bode well that midnight would be just about the perfect time to do it.

He'd also decided that the roof of Gladius House was the right place to do it. The gap from the section of roof directly above his window and the next tower-like segment was not too large. From his window, he could just reach where the two sets of eaves met, then climb up to the flat area above the wider dormer next to his. By all accounts, he needed to be out in the moonlight—well, the lack thereof—and he needed to be somewhere no one could see him. Especially with the twist on the ritual he'd decided was necessary.

Maybe he was just going nuts from missing Jess, he thought as he packed the things he would need, and had to reach down to adjust his erection in his jeans. He was harder in anticipation for this than he was on some of their dates.

The wind was chilly as he opened his window as wide as it would go and climbed up onto the adjacent roof with everything he needed in a bag slung over his shoulder.

Getting up to the little tarred square of flat roof wasn't hard at all. He knelt facing where the invisible moon should be, and began taking things out of the bag.

First he drew a circle in front of him with a mixture of powdered quartz and salt, crisscrossed by a few lines. He laid the amulet at the center of the design. Next he took out the flask of materials that had been steeping since Christmas. The scent as he uncorked it made his eyes water, but he coated his fingertips with the stuff and smeared it first on his forehead, then on the amulet itself. He felt nearly as dizzy as he had from the stuff they had been passing around on New Year's Eve.

That must mean you did it right, he thought. He blinked. Did it look like the amulet was lit for a moment there, like a beam of light had glanced across it? Or was that just something in his eye?

Whatever. Now was not the time to get distracted. He had a few more things to do, his throat getting progressively drier and the sound of the wind seeming to whistle in his ears as he finished the last few steps.

The final thing he did before beginning the actual incantation was unzip his fly and bare his cock. His fingers were still a little sticky with the tincture he'd made, but it was too late to come up with some way to clean them, and he knew from experience that wanking with his left hand was a losing proposition.

He bit down on an oath as he gave his length one experimental stroke. He didn't want to accidentally invoke any deities who weren't welcome. Better just stick to the Greek.

He began chanting the words, stroking himself in the kind of rhythm they made, and quickly falling into a kind of trance.

Somewhere in the back of his mind, as he slipped into the trance state, he was thinking again, *That means it's working.*

It was, in its way, a lot like those times when he and Jess were making love and time ceased to move forward. He only knew time was passing because he could sense the moon in motion. No, the Earth in motion. Well, both.

In most of the traditional rituals he'd read, the magic user had to have some way of drawing power together, and some way of releasing it. Since none of the things the writings had described had made sense to him—there was always a "and then you just do it" aspect—he'd decided to go with the way he thought it most likely he could do it. With sexual energy.

He was unprepared, however, for the fact that while he had been stroking himself, low clouds had been gathering in the dark, and he was definitely not ready for the nearly simultaneous clap of thunder and bolt of lightning that hit just as he was shouting out the last round of the incantation, struggling to get the last word out through gritted teeth as his orgasm tore through him.

Freezing cold rain felt like ice pellets and suddenly stung his skin, and he swore. He stuffed the amulet into his pocket and his cock into his pants, the only thought in his head that he had to get out of the storm. He was still blinking with the afterglow of the lightning strike in his eyes, and the rain was making it nearly impossible to open his eyes larger than slits.

The slanted portion of the roof was slippery. He gripped the edge of the eaves, his knuckles white.

His window looked very far away. Reaching up had been far easier than getting back to it would be. Even if he could sit on the very edge of the gutter, he couldn't get his feet all the way back onto his own sill—the gap between the two dormers was too wide.

Shit. He wasn't even sure he could get back in. But what could he do now? Even if he yelled and screamed for help, the chances of someone hearing him were slim. No one was out in the middle of the night in the storm to see him wave, and he could not spend the night on the roof in the freezing cold rain. He had to get back inside. The window was still open the way he had left it, and rain was wetting the papers on his desk, too. Leaning all the way out, he couldn't quite touch the green copper gutter above his own window, not without possibly slipping and falling four stories to the sidewalk.

He swallowed hard. If he died doing this, well, it'd probably be a baffling obituary that would run.

Kyle leaped out and grabbed the gutter, swinging his legs toward the gaping open window. A piece of the gutter came loose and he fell back, but both legs had made it through the window frame. He grabbed on by spreading his feet with a kick, one calf hooked on the window frame, the other side hooked with his foot. The vertigo was far worse, but adrenaline gave him the strength to sit all the way up and grab the frame with his hands as well and pull himself into the room.

He fell in a wet heap over the desk and onto the floor, dragging papers and loose change and miscellaneous other stuff with him, but he didn't care. God, the floor had never felt so good. He hugged it for a while.

Then he forced himself to get up and shut the window. When he collapsed again, at least it was into bed, perhaps the first time he'd been so glad that the room was that small. He was unconscious quickly after that.

He woke perhaps two hours later, supremely stiff and uncomfortable. He pulled the amulet from his pocket. Had the ritual worked? He supposed he had to wait until he met an actual siren to find out. He put it in a desk drawer and then dragged himself into a very hot shower. When he emerged from that, he fell into bed again and lost consciousness once more.

He woke again around dawn, ravenous, the wreckage strewn on the floor visible in the dim grayness evidence that he hadn't dreamed the ritual or the storm. He hoped the storm wasn't a sign that he'd failed in the ritual or an omen that he was doing the wrong thing.

It didn't feel like the wrong thing.

Hiding out in the library after hours the next night, however, that felt just the slightest bit questionable.

* * * *

Endymion
by Henry Wadsworth Longfellow

The rising moon has hid the stars;
Her level rays, like golden bars,
Lie on the landscape green,
With shadows brown between.

And silver white the river gleams,
As if Diana, in her dreams,
Had dropt her silver bow
Upon the meadows low.

On such a tranquil night as this,
She woke Endymion with a kiss,
When, sleeping in the grove,
He dreamed not of her love.

Like Dian's kiss, unasked, unsought,
Love gives itself, but is not bought;
Nor voice, nor sound betrays
Its deep, impassioned gaze.

It comes, — the beautiful, the free,
The crown of all humanity, —
In silence and alone
To seek the elected one.

It lifts the boughs, whose shadows deep
Are Life's oblivion, the soul's sleep,
And kisses the closed eyes
Of him, who slumbering lies.

O weary hearts! O slumbering eyes!
O drooping souls, whose destinies
Are fraught with fear and pain,
Ye shall be loved again!

No one is so accursed by fate,
No one so utterly desolate,
But some heart, though unknown,
Responds unto his own.

Responds,—as if with unseen wings,
An angel touched its quivering strings;
And whispers, in its song,
"Where hast thou stayed so long?"

Kyle stared at the poem. He was using his phone as a flashlight, huddled in the stacks near where he'd lost Jess that very first day she'd shown him around.

He was certain, quite certain, that he'd felt or heard something. He'd forgotten it entirely until tonight, when he'd been wandering through the dark building, wondering where the best place to tempt the siren would be. Then it had come back to him, as he'd approached the spot. Someone, or something, had touched the back of his neck, caressed his ear...

At the time he'd thought it had been Jess, playing around. The assumption that it had been her was one of the reasons he'd been bold enough to ask her out to dinner. He counted himself lucky, then, that she said yes, and that things had worked out so well between them.

But now he knew something strange was afoot in the library. His reasoning went something like this. If there was a real siren haunting the place, who stayed hidden and only revealed herself at night, if she had been the one who attacked Alex, then he wanted to catch her, and if she hadn't—well, wouldn't she know something about the attack? Dean Bell was definitely hiding something, and maybe this way Kyle could find out what.

This was, of course, all supposing that the amulet he'd made would work, and that the siren would actually emerge.

Kyle's plan was quite forgotten, however, as he found himself absorbed in the poem of Longfellow's. He had goose bumps reading it. The feeling that this one connected somehow to the first Avestan cycle was unshakable.

He took out his own notebook and began to write a commentary.

The main gist of most interpretations of the prophecy is that a great cataclysm is coming, and that only a prophesied pair of lovers can avert the disaster. It's rather unique in that you just never ever see prophecies predicting two people to exist. They're pretty much always about one individual, one king, or one hero, or whatever. But perhaps

142 × CECILIA TAN

that's a large part of why the first cycle is so popular. The implication of the lovers is that the power of love is somehow one of the qualities this pair possesses in order to save the day.

Each of the poems I've encountered and noted here, beginning with Eliot, feel to me like poetic riffs on the mystery, bringing the prophecy out of the realm of the prediction and down to the level of the personal, the characters and people to whom this great story would have happened. Or will happen to, if one believes there is any actual prediction taking place.

He heard a sound. Yes, definitely a sound. Would a siren wear boots? It was the sound of boot heels hitting the floor with a determined stride.

Kyle pressed himself under the desk at a study carrel, wondering if holding his breath would be of any help or not. Probably not. He tried to breathe very softly but couldn't do anything about how hard his heart was beating. Hopefully only he could hear that.

The boots went right past him, and the trailing hem of someone's traditional robes.

Dean Bell?

The boots went back and forth a few times. Then a voice: unmistakably Bell. "Faust's swollen left testicle." Kyle heard a thump, as if he'd banged his fist against a shelf.

The sounds of him stalking about faded. Kyle forced himself to wait a half hour crammed under the desk before he emerged, straining to hear any sound that might mean he was still in the building. But nothing and no one jumped out at him, and after another minute of standing stock still, he sat in desk chair and let out a relieved breath.

So what was Bell doing? Was he looking for the siren, too? Or something else? Whatever it was, it sounded like he didn't find it. And he didn't find Kyle either. Kyle wondered what kind of spells Bell could use to find someone. But maybe he would have had to know who he was looking for? And wasn't he supposed to have some kind of powers as dean—or assistant dean, anyway—that were supposed to let him commune with the buildings somehow? Maybe that was exaggerated. More questions Kyle wanted to ask Alex.

He seemed to be alone again, and soon grew bold enough to walk up and down the stacks again. By most accounts, a siren needed to have sex at least once a month. A true siren would think nothing of having sex with someone against their will if she needed to, though typically they were more seductresses than rapists. Their victims would think that they wanted to have sex with them. And certainly if there were one here, she would have no shortage of horny students who needed help with their exams who would offer themselves up?

Suddenly Kyle had an idea. He unzipped his fly slowly, the metallic sound of the zipper seeming to disappear this deep in the stacks.

Anxiety that Bell might swoop around the corner any second transmuted into an illicit thrill as he came quickly to full hardness. *Come on...here you go...*he thought, as if trying to coax a scared cat out from under a couch with an enticing bit of tuna.

He dropped to his knees, his shoulder bag coming to rest on the floor, as he stroked himself. When he closed his eyes, he could see the goddess Diana, bending down to bestow an unasked-for kiss on mortal lips—

His eyes flew open.

Nothing. Just his imagination. He kept stroking himself, looking around in the darkness and trying to be silent to listen, waiting to feel that phantom touch on his neck, to hear that whisper.

A half hour later, he backed down from the brink of orgasm for the umpteenth time, biting his fist. Should he stop? He didn't want to stop. He wanted to come like Mount Vesuvius. But he didn't want to make a mess, and he didn't want to give up. He could find the restroom and do it in there, but he would have to turn the light on in there to keep from just making the mess worse, and he was convinced that would somehow give him away. The wisest course of action was probably to just leave his cock alone until the erection went down, then find some corner to fall asleep in for a few hours before going back into hiding just before the building opened again in the morning.

Yeah, right. Falling asleep while as horny as Merlin's third cousin's goat sounded about as doable as levitation right now. *Alex, you pigfucking son of Circe, this is all your fault...*

The restroom it was. Using only the light from his phone he managed to make himself a large wad of toilet paper, which he used in both hands to wank himself quickly to a silent but heart-stopping orgasm. It hadn't taken long, but he felt somewhat chafed. He stuffed the wad down into a trash bin and wondered what to do next.

* * * *

Four nights later, he had seen Dean Bell twice more, but Bell had seemed unaware of his presence each time. And perhaps it was a good thing Kyle hadn't found the siren yet, since it wasn't until that fifth night that he read another account of the amulet he'd made and finally realized the siren wasn't the one who was supposed to wear the amulet at all. Of course the siren wasn't supposed to wear it! How would you get something like that around a Sphinx's neck?

Kyle looped the chain over his own neck, feeling foolish in the extreme.

A few days before term started again, students began to trickle back into the house. The dining hall reopened, which was wonderful, since the weather had continued to be nasty and slogging out once a day to see Alex had been enough of the great outdoors for Kyle's taste.

He told Alex all about making the amulet and almost breaking his neck getting back into his room, and about Bell stalking the library every other night. "I can't help but feel he has it in for you somehow," Kyle said. "At least, that was the impression you always gave me, and nothing I've seen has improved my opinion of him."

But Alex never answered. The stocking was still hanging on the window, even though it was well past the Christmas season now. Kyle didn't take it down, and neither did anyone else.

At least he had some friends to eat with and hang around in the common room with. The Glads seemed a lot more relaxed and less clique-ish when there were only a few of them around. One night Kyle and Nichols were playing cards when the door burst open and Frost came stumbling into the room, swearing about the sticking door.

Kyle chuckled under his breath, and when Frost had gone through to the stairs to his room, he remarked to Nichols, "I guess I'm not the only one who has trouble with that door."

Nichols looked at him funny but said nothing, just placed his next card on the table between them.

Kyle examined his hand, then asked, "You're a year ahead of him. How did he get ahead of you in the pecking order?"

Nichols gave Kyle another look, but one without any malice. "Well, if he hadn't rescued me on Halloween, you mean. I owe him big time for that."

"But besides that."

Nichols shrugged. "I know what you're thinking. And he's a foundling too, and not even dating someone in the house. But he always does things that gain him status. That includes top grades in all his classes, for one thing."

"But there are plenty of people who get good grades."

Nichols shrugged. "More likely people just respond, consciously or unconsciously, to the amount of power he has."

For a moment Kyle though Nichols was using the word "power" as a synonym for "status," but then realized that wouldn't make sense. "Wait. You mean magical power? How can you tell?"

Nichols winced. "Some of us can just tell. He's like...dripping with it."

"Dripping?"

"Just a metaphor. Some people sense things palpably, others see them as if they were visible to the naked eye."

"You can see how powerful he is?"

Nichols wouldn't meet Kyle's eyes. "Yeah. He glows."

Kyle had to make a conscious effort to close his mouth. "Um." And then opened it again, seizing the opportunity. "What about me?"

Nichols was forced to look up at him then. "Oh. You...not many people come close to the kind of raw power Frost has, you know."

"This isn't about me feeling inadequate next to Frost..."

"It isn't? But you were just asking me how he got such high status..."

"Nick, come on. Just tell me what I look like."

Nichols dropped his eyes again. "You're not easy to get a sense of, and sometimes you seem like you're almost not there at all, but I can't tell if that's just that you're not projecting? Your power is more like heat to me. It's kind of like there's a light bulb inside you, but when it's on, you can't actually see it, in there, but you can feel if it warms up. If I just passed you on the street I wouldn't say, there goes one of us. But that doesn't mean the power's not there. Does that make sense?"

Kyle slumped. "I guess. And I suppose to a lot of people I just...don't seem magical at all?"

Nichols shook his head. "You can't think that way. But magically speaking, I mean...you went to a normal school until you got here, right?"

"Yeah."

"Well, there was a pecking order there, too, wasn't there? How was it set? Like in gym class, someone had to be picked last for teams, right?"

"Well, you could tell some kids were more athletic than others, some were more coordinated, or they played more sports..."

"Right." Nichols folded his cards. "And the ones with the most ability tended to do the most sports, reinforcing that image. Well, magical ability is like that, too, and human nature's the same. So you've got to show what you've got sometimes, or how is anyone going to know? No one's got a very high opinion of you, but it's nothing personal if everyone else is just ahead. You started late, didn't make the dean's list, never have performed for tea or anything..."

"I'm organizing the Masque, though," Kyle put in.

"Which is good. And hanging around with Speyer helps. I never would have gotten on a broom if it hadn't been for her. Remy never would have picked me." Nichols shrugged. "Until I came here, I always was the last kid picked for teams, and I never wanted to distinguish myself academically either, because I was afraid I'd be accused of cheating and somehow this would lead to my magic being exposed...It's been kind of a challenge, learning not to be a wallflower."

"But doesn't someone have to be the wallflower?" Kyle mused out loud.

"Not in this house," Nichols answered seriously. "Honestly, though, you're doing what you can to move up. You're smart to just ignore the other freshmen. You're on a social committee with Speyer. Get Master Brandish to laugh out loud at dinner—as long as she's not laughing *at* you, that is—and you'll gain some respect from the others. If you really want to be bold, take your tray right over to Speyer's table and sit down with her. Claim Masque planning talk or whatever. If she doesn't kick you out, you're golden."

Kyle thought about it. "I really hoped I was leaving this kind of...politics behind when I left high school."

Nichols shrugged. "Human nature doesn't change. The reason the house is like this is so you can learn how to swim upstream, here where your progress is actually measured. Once you're out in the real world, you think someone will just hand you a score at the end of the day to let you know where you stand at your job or among your neighbors or whatever? There's a reason Glads tend to be in leadership positions."

Kyle sat back. "I never thought of it that way."

Now Nichols half smiled. "What, never realized this is all one big learning experience?"

"I knew that. I just didn't know it was so structured." Kyle folded his cards too, his mind no longer on the game.

"Manners, the proper way of speaking, learning to size up whether someone should be addressed as a peer or as someone of higher status...you're not going to learn that any way but living it. You especially, since you didn't grow up with it."

"And here I thought it was just arbitrary stuff to annoy us."

"Nope. So when are you and Speyer going to announce dance practice?"

"Dance practice?"

Nichols now grinned. "Oh, come on, you aren't going to hold a formal dance, a Masque especially, without making sure everyone in the house can acquit themselves properly on the dance floor?"

"Um...?"

Nichols sighed and rolled his eyes. "There will be pavanes. There will be sarabandes. There will be contra dance of all kinds.

You'll be expected to go through the courtly dances so you can meet potential partners."

"Partners?"

"It's a *masque*," Nichols said, as if that explained everything. Perhaps it did. Kyle remembered what Master Brandish had said about some in Esoteric Studies discouraging masques from being held, ostensibly because of the erotic consequences. "Right."

"Mark my words. If she doesn't make the whole house practice, she'll at least make sure anyone who doesn't know how, will."

Kyle didn't doubt that Nichols was right.

* * * *

The night Jess returned, even a run-in with Frost couldn't bring Kyle's mood down. In the Gladius dining hall, Kyle had seen him eating alone. As he'd passed by him, he'd tried to be civil.

"You're looking well, Frost," he said. Frost's cheeks almost looked like they had some color. "Did you go somewhere warm for break?"

But Frost had just glared at him and replied with a sneer, "Nowhere special, but it beat staying here, I bet."

Whatever. He was probably cranky because he and Candlin hadn't seen each other in weeks. Kyle could understand that; he'd been pretty moody himself while Jess had been gone. He grinned at Frost, pretending like Frost hadn't said anything. "Well, enjoy dessert. I'm off to meet up with Jess," he said, then sauntered away, quite sure Frost was staring daggers into his back.

When Kyle got to Camella House, she was standing on the front step, and a month's worth of anxiety melted away as she came running up to him before he could even reach her, grabbed him in a huge hug, and kissed him. Through their winter coats it was a bulky hug, but to Kyle that just made it seem all the warmer.

"I missed you, too," he said.

"Come on, let's go get coffee and you can tell me all about what you did while I was gone," she said with a grin.

He laughed and they began walking hand in hand toward the Square. "You mean you can tell me what you did, since all I did was sit around, mope and study."

"Was it really that bad?"

"Just boring, mostly. I'll tell you about it once we get settled."

They ended up with hot chocolate instead of coffee, and a table in the cramped back corner of the coffee shop where their knees touched. Kyle didn't mind at all. He held his chocolate in both hands, feeling like the heat from it soaked through his whole body from his palms, and listened to her tell stories about her various family members, and the new CD she bought, and a few movies she saw.

When she wound down, he told her he'd been visiting Alex every day, that nothing was different other than he was starting to look kind of skinny, and about how he'd started reading the commentaries for some of the prophecies, which led him to trying to figure out how not to tell her how much trouble he'd had conjuring.

But eventually he got down to the part about the library. "I looked for the siren," he said quietly, realizing it suddenly sounded like a much stupider and less impressive thing to do than he'd hoped it would.

Especially when Jess seemed less than thrilled. "You what?"

"I didn't find her," he said quietly. "Er, it. I did spend the night in the library a couple of times and there's no siren there. If there is, she...it's really hiding from everyone. But Dean Bell was there."

"Dean Bell caught you in the library?"

"No, no. I saw him a few times, like he was looking for the siren, too, and didn't find anything. Me included."

She frowned. "Kyle, you could have gotten into huge trouble. Or worse, what if you *had* found the siren, or the siren found you? You could have ended up like Alex. And if you're trying to keep your options open, as far as Esoteric Studies goes..." She made a face. "A siren fucking you...it still counts as sex."

"Oh." Kyle hadn't thought about it that way. "Well, but I'm not sure I..." He paused mid-sentence, his brain catching up to his mouth. No, he wasn't sure if Esoteric Studies was something he wanted to go into, but then again, his big discovery of the past few weeks had been that masturbating and magic seemed to go hand in hand for him. "Well, I wasn't looking for her to have sex," he said a bit more defensively.

Jess made a frustrated noise. "That wouldn't matter to a siren. If they want to have you, you don't get much choice."

"Well..." He took a breath and then pulled the chain out from under his shirt to show her the amulet. "I made this. It should keep me from getting attacked by sirens. And Sphinxes."

"Sphinxes are extinct," she said offhandedly, lifting the amulet in her palm and frowning as she examined it. "Where did you get this?"

"Um, well, the necklace came from a clothing shop around the corner. The one where you said everything's ugly?" He pointed vaguely in the direction of the place. "I researched the spell for a couple of weeks."

She sat back. "Wow. And does it work?" She seemed less annoyed now and he took that as a good sign.

"Hard to say, since I don't think I've met any sirens or part-sirens since making it. No one's been here, after all." He shrugged.

She ran her fingers down his cheek. "You've really been lonely, haven't you?"

He just nodded, closing his eyes as she traced his eyebrows with her fingertips. He swallowed, realizing two desires were at war inside him. One side wanted Monica to be there tonight, so he could test out whether she was a siren or not. The other side hoped she wasn't there, so he and Jess could get reacquainted. "Monica?" he asked.

"Got back an hour before me," Jess said, sounding a little wistful herself.

"I've been having dreams about you." He tilted his chin forward for a quick kiss.

"I'll find out when she's in lab next, okay?" She ran her hand up his thigh. "Can you hold out until then?"

"Not if you keep touching me like th—" His breath caught as her other hand slid warmly up his other thigh and he realized the wicked gleam in her eye meant she knew exactly what effect she was having on him. "Jess..."

She leaned forward to whisper in his ear. "I haven't got off in a month. I touched myself a few times, thinking of you...but...it just wasn't the same."

Kyle wasn't sure which of them moved first, but it felt like they'd just agreed on their plan of action. He returned their mugs to the bin while she got the key to the restroom. He followed a few moments after her, to the back hall where the two doors were. He tried the handle of the one marked "Women" and it opened. She latched the door behind him, and a moment later he had her pressed against the wall by a hungry kiss.

She had hung her coat on the hook on the back of the door, but he didn't even remove his from his shoulders as he turned her in his arms, undoing her slacks and pushing them down along with her underwear. He got his own jeans down to his knees and rubbed his bare cock against the cleft of her ass. She pushed back against him, urging him on.

He kept one arm around her while he slicked his cock with spit and slipped it into the crook of her thighs. She leaned forward, holding onto the handicapped safety bar, making it easier for him to move his cock and to get a nice deep-feeling thrust. He needn't have worried about friction; she was quite slippery.

"How's this?" he breathed, pushing her forward and pulling her back on his prick. "Am I hitting you—?"

The noise she made when the head of his cock rubbed her clit left no room for doubt and no reason to hold back. Kyle began moving with short, quick thrusts, and Jess stifled a moan. When he felt like she was getting close, he reached his hand around and spread her lips just enough to get his middle finger right onto her clit. Now he lengthened his thrusts, seeking the rhythm and stimulation that would bring him off quickly, even as his finger worked to finish the job his cockhead had started.

When she came she wasn't able to keep completely quiet, nor was he, as her muscles clenching sent him over the edge, too, spurting messily onto the wall and dribbling a little down her thighs.

Nothing that some paper towels and some water couldn't clean up. They rearranged themselves quickly, only slowing down for one moment for Kyle to bury his nose in her hair and take a deep breath of her scent. "I missed you."

They emerged cautiously, but no one was standing in line, and Jess dropped the key off at the register as she breezed out. They were still a little red-faced from exertion when they kissed good-bye at the door of Camella House.

It wasn't until Kyle's post-orgasmic haze lifted somewhat that he realized he still hadn't tested the amulet on Monica. It would have to be next time.

* * * *

Nichols didn't have to be prophetic to be right about Caitlyn Speyer. She organized a practice for the afternoon of the Saturday before classes started and Kyle found himself in the common room shuffling his feet with a couple of other nervous freshmen while a few of the upperclassmen explained how the dancing worked.

"Three, count 'em, three. I expect you each to dance a minimum of three times," Caitlyn said, stalking up and down their ranks like a military sergeant. "If you only master one of the dances, you'll have to wait until it comes around again. No doubt some of the others won't know how to dance either, in which case it'll be your job to walk them through it. We'll start with the pavane, which is slow and not that hard to figure out."

As it turned out, Caitlyn herself didn't have the patience to teach the steps. She'd delegated that to others. Remy took Kyle's group and began to explain, while the students who had done it before were walked through the paces by Caitlyn and Masterson.

They weren't evenly split girls and boys among the freshmen and others who had never danced this way before, so Kyle found himself face to face with a ruddy-cheeked guy with dirty blond hair down to his shoulders. He'd seen him a thousand times around the house of course, but couldn't remember his name. Hopefully he'd remember it before he had cause to use it.

The pavane wasn't that hard. Soon they were mixed in with the students who knew how it went, and another student whose name Kyle couldn't remember played a small frame drum to keep them in time.

They moved on to other dances, then, and with more intricate changes of partner. Kyle wondered if it was going to be even more confusing when everyone was wearing masks. He was just wondering this as Caitlyn herself stepped into place beside him and they turned to press their palms together.

She pulled her hand back suddenly, "Circe's tit!" She shook it like she had been shocked by a massive jolt of static electricity, but Kyle hadn't felt anything. "Wadsworth, what...?"

Kyle's eyes were wide. Did Caitlyn have siren blood? If so, she might not want everyone in the room to know about it. "Er, sorry," he said. "Shuffling my feet on the carpet." He shook his own hand, too, belatedly.

"Well, pick them up a bit more, and quit wearing those polyester pants," she shot back, but he could see she was just playing along. They mimed their way through the dance without actually touching.

When the dance practice was over, she cornered him in private near the back door to the kitchen. "So what the fuck was that? I've never got a jolt like that off you before."

"Um, you don't by any chance have any mantic blood?" Kyle asked.

"What do you mean, mantic blood? My mother's a seer, if that's what you're asking."

"Er, mantic, I mean like Sphinxes and sirens," Kyle amended.

Caitlyn scowled at him. "You know mantic is a synonym for prophetic, right?"

"It is? I, um, I learned it from a book. I'd been assuming it was related to the manticore..." He broke off when she made a derisive sound.

"Get to the point, Wadsworth. Why did you shock me?"

"I didn't mean to. I asked about mantic creature ancestry because of this." He pulled the amulet out of his shirt. "It's supposed to give me the power to make Sphinxes tell the truth."

"Sphinxes are..."

"Extinct, I know. But it should work on other 'mantic creatures,' or so I read." He put it back under the cloth and the amulet felt chilly against his skin, just from that. "Sirens included. I was trying to find the one in the library."

Caitlyn folded her arms. "Well, there have been a lot of seers in my family. It's possible we've got a siren somewhere back in the family tree. But that's probably true of everyone here—well, not sirens specifically, but various magical beings. I know not everyone believes that, but...well. You need to be more careful."

"I'm sorry. I didn't mean to..."

"It's all right, Wadsworth, I'm sure I'm not hurt. But if you've got a thing with that kind of power, you just have to be really careful with it." She took a half step back. "If it's something that controls mantic power, that's some powerful stuff. Sphinxes weren't exactly pushovers, you know."

"Yeah, I know." He sighed.

But he didn't quit wearing the amulet. He was afraid it would get lost or stolen if he put it in his desk drawer or hid it somewhere, and he just tried to be careful about not touching people. That night he and Jess had a normal date, but of course that meant Monica was off at her lab and he had no chance to test it on her. He stopped by just to socialize a few times over the next few days but never saw her, but with classes having started that Monday, he was already beginning to feel pressed for time. And there were only two weeks until the date of the Masque, with dancing practice, and mask-making, and homework.

Meanwhile Kyle's love poem for Jess remained unwritten. She came to Tea with the Master again, though, at which Kyle recited a poem that was not specifically about her, but which seemed to go over well, and the only annoying thing about the positive response he got was that Frost was not there to see it. "I wonder where the little kiss-ass is," he murmured to Jess at one point during dessert. "He usually never misses a chance like this."

But after folks had dispersed and Kyle was standing in front of the house with Jess, saying goodbye to her, the front door burst open and the guy with the apple cheeks whose name Kyle still had not remembered since dance practice came running out.

"Oh good, you're still here." He looked back and forth between Kyle and Jess.

Jess blinked. "Um, have we met?"

He swallowed, catching his breath, and then nodding his head. "Persephon Cavendish. Most people call me Persy. I was there Halloween night. I, um, you have to help my roommate. He won't..." He swallowed again, and Kyle realized his short-ness of breath was probably because he was panicking and not because of running after them. "He won't wake up."

"Circe's tit," Jess said, and shooed him back into the house, hurrying behind him.

Kyle went with them, back through the common room, where a few heads turned as they went through, but no one seemed to know anything was amiss. It wasn't until Persy pushed open the door to his room that Kyle felt the urgency of the situation himself.

Persy's roommate was none other than Timothy Frost, who was lying on his bed atop the covers, his hands folded on his stomach and his eyes wide open, looking for all the world like a corpse.

Jess put a hand on his head. "Frost?"

He was unresponsive. Limp. She sat on the edge of the low bed, her palm on his forehead and her eyes closed for a few moments.

"He was just like this when you found him?" Kyle asked.

"Yes," Persy said in a weak voice. "There are no marks or anything, doesn't look like he fell and hit his head..."

Jess opened her eyes. "He needs someone with more Heal-ing Arts than me. Get Master Brandish."

Persy stood paralyzed.

"I'll go," Kyle said. Persy made a kind of whimper of protest, but didn't actually do anything to stop him.

Kyle took the stairs two at a time and found the Master chat-ting with two students outside the door of her apartment. It took only moments before she was rushing back up to Frost and Cavendish's room, and only a few moments more for everyone in the house, it seemed, to know what was going on. Brandish emerged from the room, carrying Frost in her arms, and ordered everyone to their own rooms immediately. "I don't think it's an attack," she stressed, "but for safety, please, everyone to your rooms. Remy, a headcount by the time I return."

So Kyle watched from his own window to see her carrying him across the campus, Frost looking small and wan in her arms, his eyes still staring, unseeing.

"Kyle."

He nearly jumped out of his skin at the sound of his name right there in the room with him, but he recognized the voice.

He whirled around and there was Alex, looking somewhat frail and wrung out, but alive and awake.

"Holy crap, Alex, what the hell are you doing here?"

Alex's smile was somewhat crooked. "You came to visit me every day. I figured it was about time I returned the favor." Under his jacket, he was still wearing the loose hospital pajamas and had square marks on his arms where tubes and things had been taped down. He was barefoot and there was no sign of his shoes. "I've been waiting for you to get back from tea."

"Alex..." Kyle was overjoyed to see him, but at the same time, confused. "What's going on?"

Alex sat on the edge of the bed and Kyle sat next to him. "I'm afraid to go back to my room," Alex said simply.

"Why?"

"Because Monica might be there."

"I knew it!" Kyle leaped to his feet. "I've been suspecting her since the night you were attacked."

Alex's eyebrows shot up in surprise. "You have?"

But Kyle waved at him to keep talking. "Tell me what happened."

Alex took a deep breath. "Well, you probably know a lot of this. But...I went to the library and got myself locked in on purpose. I was getting desperate and, you know, may as well see if the siren rumor was true, right? If it wasn't, well, at least I spent the night studying and all that.

"I was walking through the stacks. It wasn't that late yet. All of a sudden I turned around and she was there." Alex looked behind him as if she might appear in Kyle's room, too. "I was like, 'oh wow, Monica, you're the siren? Well, I'm sorry I didn't take you up on your offer sooner, then, would have saved me a lot of trouble.'

"Maybe that was the wrong thing to say. She launched herself at me, her hands turning into like giant bird talons or something." He rubbed at his collarbone where Kyle knew there was a scar. "That's the last thing I remember, really." Then he rubbed his forehead. "She tore into my mind, too, not just my skin. I gather I've been out for more than two months?"

"It's February. Term just started a few days ago," Kyle said. "Don't you think you should go to Dean Bell with this? He's been unable to figure out who did it or to catch them."

Alex shook his head. "You know they'll come up with some way for it to be my fault." He heaved a heavy sigh. "I bet they'll blame Frost on me, too."

"Frost? How?"

"I mysteriously wake up from a coma at the same time he falls into one? I guarantee I'll get blamed." Alex shook his head, then looked back at Kyle. "I'm starved."

Kyle needed to think. He needed to sit down and sort out all the new information, but there were more urgent things to take care of. "Do you have your room key? I'll go to your place and get you some clothes and stuff. I'll bring back food, too."

Alex felt in his coat pockets, then broke out into a smile. "Here they are." He pulled his keys from his pocket.

"You'll be safe here until I get back, won't you?"

Alex took a look around. "The place is pretty defensible, yeah."

"No, I mean, if she comes after you. You don't think Monica's actually responsible for Frost, do you?"

Alex blanched. "Maybe it *is* my fault. Maybe she was coming after me and ran into him..."

Kyle shook his head. "Here, this will keep you safe from Monica." He took the amulet off and put it over Alex's head. "It's an amulet that will make Sphinxes and sirens tell you the truth. And presumably not bite your head off in one gulp, either. Sphinxes were no pushovers."

Alex ran his fingers over the amulet. "Um, okay. Why were you wearing it?"

"Because I've been trying to catch the siren. I haven't seen Monica since I made it, though."

"Maybe she knows what it is and she's been hiding from you because of it?" Alex lay back on Kyle's bed, holding the amulet up in his hand so he could look at it.

"Dunno. Be back as quick as I can."

Kyle hurried across the quad to Camella House. Lindy and Yoshi were watching TV when he came into the suite. He just waved and went to Alex's room, packed up some things in a bag, then exited, locking the door behind him.

"Monica around?" he asked, as he came back into the suite.

"I think she's taking a nap," Lindy said. "You off to visit Alex or something?"

"Yeah," Kyle said. "Just bringing him some things. You never know what might help someone wake up."

"You never do," Lindy agreed. "Good luck. I haven't gone to see him since I got back from break."

"Sure. Later." Kyle hurried down the stairs, then into the Square where he spent his last five dollars on a sandwich he hoped someone who had been eating nothing but pumped-in liquids for two months could digest.

Alex wolfed down the tuna sandwich like a man who hadn't eaten since Thanksgiving. "You have to keep it a secret that I'm here," Alex said, between bites. "You can't even tell Jess. Sirens can read minds, you know? She'd find out."

"Lindy said she was there, but taking a nap," Kyle said. "Could she be tired out from attacking Frost?"

Alex licked his fingers thoughtfully. "Hmm. Usually a siren gets energy from the people she has sex with. But maybe it has to be 'digested' like food? Could be. Speaking of which..."

He was asleep before Kyle could even say anything. Kyle nudged him over onto his back and pulled the blanket over him. If sirens could read minds, then Kyle really had to make sure he didn't go near Monica unless he was wearing the amulet. In fact, it was probably best if he didn't confront her until he could be sure that he could get her to confess in front of a Judge like Dean Bell.

He lay down next to Alex on the narrow bed, trying to imagine the circumstances where Bell and Monica would be in the same place. "Well," he said to Alex's sleeping form, "looks like my dance card at the Masque is going to be full."

February

A WEEK into February, Kyle thought maybe his head was going to explode. He wasn't used to keeping a secret, for one thing, and Alex living in his room was a pretty huge one. It meant sneaking food to him constantly, and worrying about what would happen if they were caught. The morning after Alex had appeared, there had been quite a ruckus over his disappearance from the Healing Arts building, especially since Frost was now in essentially the same situation Alex had been in. Kyle didn't think Alex would have been blamed for anything relating to Frost if he'd just gone to the PTBs right away, but after mysteriously disappearing into the night?

On top of that, there were all the preparations for the Masque, continued failed attempts at writing a love poem for Jess, actually skipping a date with her with worry over running into Monica and accidentally revealing Alex's existence. Then there was the fact that his Magical Biology class made no sense. He sat at his desk trying to write a paper on the parallels of mundane taxonomy to magical, only to find himself basically arguing that magical taxonomy made no sense.

"Something wrong, Ace?" Alex asked from the bed, where he was reading a comic book.

"What makes you ask?" Kyle said without looking up from his notes.

"Oh, the fact that you just about bit that pencil in half."

"Oh." Kyle set it down and sighed. "It's just that Magical Biology isn't biology at all. It's not science. If it was, then...well, then creatures like the Sphinx couldn't exist."

"But the Sphinx did exist."

"I know," Kyle said miserably. "But I can't make it make sense in my head."

Alex sat up. "What doesn't make sense?"

"Well, things like the classification system." Kyle angled his desk chair so that he faced the bed. "It's a lot like how mundane science used to try to group things together, but once we looked at their DNA, we knew that, for example, some species of plant that look a lot like other plants aren't actually related at all, while others that look different were actually more closely related."

Alex crossed his legs and leaned his elbows on his knees. "What you're saying is that science gets at some underlying truth. But is it more useful?"

"What do you mean, useful? Of course science is useful."

"But you're talking about a classification system. Is it useful to know this plant that has three leaves is related to this plant that doesn't, and this other plant with three leaves is something else? Or is there something about three-leafed-ness that is actually good to know? In the case of plants with three leaves, okay, maybe that's too broad an example. But say you're talking about jaguars and leopards, for example. Both are spotted cats that evolved separately, the jaguar in South America and the leopard in Africa and Asia. If you grew up fearing the leopard, and you went to South America and saw a jaguar and reacted as if it were a leopard? You'd have done the right thing. Regardless of the fact they aren't the same animal at all, scientifically speaking."

Kyle thought about that for a moment. "You're saying the inherent truth is...?"

"That predators can eat you. And maybe the existence of two independently evolving spotted cats that can both eat you expresses some inner truth about the aesthetic of the universe. Science may prefer to classify based on ancestry and the past. Perhaps magic prefers to classify by the results, by the future."

"That makes a kind of emotional sense, but no actual sense."

"Why isn't emotional sense actual sense?" Alex sat up straighter. "In magic, emotional sense is possibly more important than actual sense. Common sense says I can't make objects levitate either." Alex made some paper clips on Kyle's desk fly across the room slowly like a tiny flock of geese and land on the bed. "We're talking about the ability to transform reality, Kyle. Science is about measuring and understanding reality. That's admirable. But magic is exactly the realm that picks up where science has to leave off. The chimera and the Sphinx and the manticore and the gryphon didn't evolve from a common ancestor. But don't you think, just looking at them, that they belong in the same category? What's the usefulness of a classification system anyway? Does it help you know what to do if you run into one on the street?"

"Well, no, since they're all extinct." Kyle sighed. "Why are all these creatures extinct, anyway?"

"They're not all extinct," Alex said. "A lot of them did die off around a thousand years ago. I'm sure your class will get into the theories on why, though no one exactly knows."

Kyle snorted. "Perhaps if they'd been more scientific at the time, we'd have an explanation."

Alex laughed quietly. "Just hope it doesn't happen again, because we'd be next." He gathered up the paper clips. "Now that I've distracted you thoroughly from your studying, care to discuss our plans for the ambush?"

"The ambush" was what they had been calling the plan to try to get Monica to confess at the Masque.

"I've been thinking," Alex went on, "that getting Bell into the right place at the right time is the most likely failure point in the plan. Once you touch Monica, she ought to be in your thrall if I've read the spell correctly, so all you have to do is get into a dance group with her. But we need the dean to hear what she says before he decides to put 'the Whammy' on me."

Alex had taken to calling the Geas "the Whammy" partly to make fun of Kyle, but Kyle had a feeling Alex needed to make fun of the Geas itself. Make light of his fears.

"Even masked, he might pick me out, so it can't be me who gets him into place. We need someone else."

Kyle thought about that. "Is there someone we can use without telling them the whole story? Or do we need to find someone we can trust with the whole plan?"

Alex frowned. "Do you have someone in mind?"

"What about telling someone I'm trying to catch the person who hurt Frost and leave you out of the story entirely? The two people I can think of who would want Frost's attacker caught most are Candlin and Cavendish."

"Hm, the boyfriend and the roommate. That has some possibilities."

"Well, and Master Brandish, but I don't think she'd take well to being duped."

"No, indeed not. Though you're right, like a lioness with her cubs." Alex's eyes brightened. "And she does have a history with the dean..."

"No," Kyle said. "We just ruled her out. She'll see through it too easily and she won't approve of us taking things into our own hands, either."

"Damn. All right, which one then: Michael or Persy?"

Kyle considered for a long moment. "I don't know."

"Which one does your gut tell you? Forget science for a minute."

"Hmm, Persy."

"Okay, now ask why."

" Because he's dumb enough to play along with what we say without delving into it deeply. Michael's too smart. He'd ask too many questions."

"Just so. Besides, Persy is here in your own house, which means you could go talk to him right now, instead of having to engineer a time to get Michael alone."

Kyle nodded and got to his feet. Michael was rarely alone, although without Frost at his side he looked rather bereft. But Marigold and Kate seemed to feel it was their duty to make sure he didn't get lonely—or maybe they were just happy to be with their friend without his pill of a boyfriend around. "I'll go talk to Persy now."

"That's the way, Ace."

* * * *

The night of the Masque arrived the following week, far too quickly for Kyle's taste, and yet it seemed to come so slowly because of how much dread he felt. But when the day actually came, he felt the dread lift. Tonight he would do it all. Save Alex, expose the siren and while flush with triumph, make Jess's dream come true with a silent request to dance, at the end of which he would conjure the first of the traditional courtship gifts—a gold coin—and formally ask for the right to court her.

But first he had to get his stockings on. He sat on the edge of the bed with Alex giggling at him, trying in vain to get his feet through. "Why do I always end up in these flimsy things on cold nights?"

Alex took pity on him. "How did you get that Batman costume on? Seriously, like this, Kyle."

He sat down and pulled off his own tights, then put them back on, demonstrating the technique of gathering the whole leg together, putting his foot directly against the toe seam, then pulling the tights up his legs. "See? Like magic."

Kyle grumbled and emulated him and the tights went on. Over that, breeches, shirt and vest, jacket, and finally mask. Everyone from Gladius House was in black and white, with silver and gold accents, and at the mask-making night they had all made more masks than they would need for the entire house to wear. It had been easy to get an extra one for Alex. Kyle checked his reflection in the bathroom mirror in the hall and hardly recognized himself.

He didn't recognize Alex either, who had slicked his hair back into a club, which made his hair look much darker and changed the shape of his face. So did the seriousness of his expression. When he added a three-quarter face mask atop that, he could have been anybody.

They made their way down the stairs together, along with other housemates heading in the same direction, and Kyle found most of them hard to recognize. He could tell Caitlyn Speyer by her laugh, though, somewhere ahead of them as they crossed the yard headed toward Lowell House. It was a clear night, just a few streaks of clouds, and for February the wind felt strangely balmy, above freezing. Kyle still wished for some of that Red Heat from Halloween, though.

One of the first people he saw on walking into the hall was a tall, courtly warrior, wearing a sword. Then with a start he realized it was Master Brandish. He wondered if that was *the* sword, or if it was only for show.

The crowd was more colorful than he had been expecting after all the monochrome of the Glads, but no other house co-ordinated colors. There were people in purple and emerald and scarlet, some in head-to-toe gold, others in fabrics that seemed to change color with the light. A group of musicians was on a riser at one end of the room, playing the traditional tunes, loud enough to energize the dancers but not so loud that those not dancing could not flirt verbally. The entire place was lit softly, the chandeliers overhead giving off champagne-colored light, and large stands of candles in tall glasses placed along the walls.

Alex caught sight of Persy and tapped Kyle on the shoulder. Yes, there he was, and Dean Bell was not far from him. Persy looked to be on task. Kyle did a slow circuit of the room but he didn't see Jess or Monica yet. He knew Jess would be in a green satin gown, with her hair up and some kind of pearls woven in it. She'd text-messaged him to say so, but hadn't sent a picture. He'd never come up with a polite way of asking *so, and what is your roommate wearing?*

A half hour passed with no sign of them. He was intimidat-ed by glares from Caitlyn to get into a dance, which he found actually helped to calm his nerves when he didn't make any major mistakes. As he was going along, he thought he saw Jess in the crowd of people watching, but when the dance was over and he went back to where she might have been, she had either moved on or it had been someone else in a green dress.

At last, though, he spotted Monica, entering with Kate and Marigold and Michael. It was Michael he recognized first, small in stature and only wearing a domino of a mask, his silk-fine black hair hanging straight down as always. In that context, Kate and Marigold were easy to identify, and he realized that it had to be Monica with them, by the streaks in her hair. Her dress was red with gold accents, too.

He began making his way toward them, not to greet them just yet, but to be ready if they jumped into a dance. All he had to do was make sure he got into the line that would meet Monica's. He would have her enthralled before she could step away.

He caught Alex's eye and Alex nodded. He would check on Persy. Kyle watched his progress across the room and Alex paused briefly by the punch bowl. Yes, there was Persy, who seemed to have received the sign as he then approached the dean and struck up a conversation.

Kyle looked for the group with Monica and Michael again. Was that Jess? Someone in a green dress was talking to someone who might have been Nichols, but without seeing her eyes, Kyle couldn't be sure. They bowed to each other and moved toward the dance floor, but following them was impossible. Just then Kyle saw the girls were dragging Michael into the dance that was just forming up, too. Kyle felt a little sorry for him. He probably would rather be sitting at Frost's bedside right now than attending a party, but it appeared his self-appointed guardians were going to force him to have some fun.

Judging by the music, this would be one of the faster dances. Kyle couldn't remember the name now, but it was one where people would turn from one partner to the other and clasp hands. Which was good, but he was nervous about screwing up the fast-paced dance. Too late to worry about that. He had to jump in now. Persy was already talking to Bell, and the lines were forming quickly. He hurried to take a place just a few people down and across from Marigold. Michael stood next to her, and Monica just on his other side.

The practice lessons must have sunk in, because Kyle found himself going along thinking much more about Monica than about what his feet were doing. Two more exchanges and he would pass between her and Michael, taking their hands as he swung through. He prepared himself to act right away. Who knew if there would be a shock like when he'd touched Caitlyn Speyer? He couldn't hesitate. He and Alex had already discussed what words to use, what were most likely to work...

The drumbeats seemed to slow, the candle flames to flicker visibly as he came closer and closer to her, turning Marigold and then bowing to her as the steps carried them on, catching a glimpse of Persy's apple cheeks at the edge of the spectators.

He took hold of Michael and Monica's hands at the same moment and felt a surge like electricity tingle through his arms—not painful, but he was glad he'd been ready for it.

"Siren, reveal yourself!"

Monica's face registered shock and puzzlement and she tried to pull her hand free. What was he supposed to say if she resisted? Oh, right.

"On your knees."

Her eyes went wide, but then so did Kyle's as Michael Candlin fell to his knees, clutching onto Kyle's wrist with his other hand.

The flow of the dancers was disrupted, and the music ground to a halt as Kyle stared into Michael's eyes, trying to remember what he was supposed to say now.

"Wadsworth, what is the meaning of this?" Bell loomed somewhere behind them, but it was like everyone in the room crowding around them had turned to just a blur, and all Kyle could see was the black-haired boy, biting his lip and fighting back tears.

"I...I've caught the siren," Kyle said. "Isn't that right?"

Michael nodded. "Yes."

Kyle could hear Alex's voice. "Are you the one who attacked me?"

Michael didn't answer. Kyle asked. "Are you the one who attacked Alex in the library?"

"Yes." Michael's teeth were gritted, as if he were fighting answering, but couldn't help himself. "Yes, I did."

"Why?"

"Because he wanted Timothy." Michael's cheeks were as scarlet as if revealing such intimate secrets were embarrassing. Kyle supposed it was. Apparently, even sirens could be mortified—and jealous. "I didn't mean to hurt him! I mean, I did, at the time I wanted to kill him, but I hadn't intended to..."

Kyle still didn't understand, though. "But then what happened to Frost? If it wasn't you?"

Kyle was the one feeling mortified now as Candlin burst into tears and sobbed against the back of his hand. "It *was* me! I didn't mean to do that, either! He was...he was always willing..." He choked on his tears for a moment before he could go on. "I just...took too much. I'd waited, the whole break, to see him again...but I waited too long. I couldn't...I c-couldn't..."

He dissolved in tears again, squeezing his eyes shut, and Kyle found himself able to look around. Master Brandish and Dean Bell were both standing to one side of him, Alex to the other, his mask in his hand. His heart did a little flip when he saw Jess was there, too, in the ring of people surrounding them. Jess, and Marigold, and Nichols, and Monica, who looked horrified. Kyle was relieved it hadn't been her. "Um, you heard all that, I assume?" Kyle said to the dean.

Bell nodded. Then got down on one knee, turning Michael to face him with his fingers on his chin. "Are you willing to help us restore Frost? I make no promise of leniency if you do."

Michael nodded. "I would. I will."

"Wadsworth, we'll need your help, too, since I do not believe Candlin here can be trusted. His intentions are trustworthy, but his appetites are not." Bell turned to look up at Brandish. "You know better than I what other assistance we will need."

Master Brandish's hand tightened on her sword. She spoke quietly, leaning toward Bell, but Kyle could hear the words perfectly where he was. "You're talking about a *resartum* of soul and body..."

"When his heart's broken. I know." Bell sounded grim. "Let's discuss this further in my office."

She nodded, then with a word cleared a path to the door. Bell barked more orders and Kyle saw Master Zoltan urging the musicians to resume playing.

Kyle pulled Michael to his feet and followed, not letting go of his hand. He kept his eyes fixed on Brandish's back, not completely sure what they were supposed to be doing next, only that they needed him to keep Michael in line. Perhaps once they got there, he could give the amulet to Bell and leave them to do whatever it was they needed to. There were people walking with them. Jess and Alex. Marjory. Dean Bell.

To Kyle it felt like a dream, this strange parade across the campus to Peyntree Hall.

When they arrived, Kyle was not surprised to see Ms. Finch and Master Lester standing on the stairs waiting for them, nor to find that inside Bell's spacious office, Frost was laid out on the couch, unconscious and looking paler than ever. There was a whole sitting area, large enough for Dean Bell to receive a dozen guests, and beyond that the imposing desk, and more room behind that, of which Kyle got only a vague sense.

Master Brandish unbuckled her sword and then knelt by Frost, stroking his forehead. "So you were draining him all along," she said to Michael. "Were you giving him back knowledge, or was your exchange one-sided?"

Michael didn't need to be compelled to answer. "He didn't need my help! He's brilliant on his own. He loves me..."

Brandish turned and fixed him with a glare. "You were attracted to him because of how powerful he is. You figured you could feed from him often without anyone noticing."

"At first! I didn't think we were going to fall in love. I thought we'd just...you know." Michael's shoulders slumped. "Once I fell in love with him, I didn't want anyone else, either. I only stalked the library because I had to. He wasn't enough."

"Callendra, let me have a look." Ms. Finch took Master Brandish's place and put her hand on Frost's forehead.

Dean Bell looked Kyle up and down. "How are you doing it?"

"Oh, um, this. It's actually meant to work on Sphinxes." Kyle pulled the amulet out from under his shirt. "I read about it first in a book of Bessarion's. Well, a translation into English, that is. Which Bessarion supposedly had passed down from Xenophon's era..."

"Yes, yes." Bell waved him to silence with an annoyed look on his face. "Sphinxes. Why didn't I think of that?"

Brandish put a hand on Bell's shoulder but he shrugged it off before she could speak. "Callendra," he said, "please tell me this *resartum* is doable."

Brandish spoke quietly. "We won't need the siren, but we will need both partners to be virgins, ideally a madonna or a brigid, and a lightning rod."

"I'm a brigid," Kyle heard Jess say from behind him in a timid voice. He turned and there she was, her mask gone but still in her green gown, as Nichols's hands tightened possessively around her waist.

He stared. "Jess, what...?"

"And Kyle's a lightning rod," Alex added, his hand on his chin.

"I am? What...?"

Several people were all talking at once then, and near as Kyle could tell they were arguing over whether he and Jess could, should, or would do what was necessary to save Frost. "Hang on, hang on!" Kyle found himself shouting. "Nobody is doing anything until I get an explanation that I can understand!"

"Sit." Bell rubbed his eyes with the fingers of one hand. "Everyone sit. I certainly hope Frost will last long enough for us to bring Mr. Wadsworth up to speed. Wadsworth, I believe you may let go of Candlin's hand. Now, he will obey you."

Kyle sat in a chair next to the couch where Frost was lying and let go of Michael's hand. Michael sat at his feet, which Kyle thought was weird, but he had enough other things to worry about that he didn't say anything. Master Brandish took the chair by Frost's head and glared at Michael.

Kyle looked back at Jess, who had settled between Nichols and Marjory on the opposite sofa, her hand held tight between both of Nichols's in his lap. She looked around at the people there and shook her head sadly. "I'm sorry, Kyle—this wasn't how I wanted to tell you. But...it's happened. My dream. He's the one."

"Oh." Kyle felt the floor shift under him, as if the entire building were being jolted sideways by an earthquake. No one else seemed to notice, though, so it must have been just him. "Wow. That's really...huh."

"Kyle had a feeling you were going to find your true love at the Masque," Alex said helpfully to Jess. "Fate's a funny old thing, isn't it?"

Master Brandish spoke. "Whether Wadsworth and Torralva are romantically involved or not doesn't really matter to me, except as it pertains to whether either or both of them would participate in the *resartum*."

"A sex magic ritual," Bell clarified, examining Kyle critically. "One that will require intercourse. 'Brigid' is a term used in Healing Arts for a female practitioner who has the gift of healing touch. I understand, Miss Torralva, that you have done this before?"

"She has," Nichols spoke up. "She healed me on Halloween. From a serious head injury."

"This is Timothy Frost's heart we're talking about, though," Ms. Finch spoke up. "His soul, his mind..."

"We're aware of that, Madeleine," Brandish said. "I'd normally say the chances of us finding a brigid who was still a virgin were one in ten thousand, yet we have one here in the room. Miss Torralva, the question is whether you are willing. I understand you are going to declare your major in Healing Arts, in which case you needn't preserve your virgin state any longer...?"

Jess cleared her throat, and Kyle felt his own ache. She looked so beautiful sitting there. "I'm willing. I've been thinking for a long time I should go into Healing Arts, but honestly, I've been holding off, you know, just in case something like this might come up."

"If only more families would imbue that kind of respect for the rites of passage..." Bell said, mostly to himself.

"So, yes," Jess said, her neck looking very long and regal as she sat up straight. "I'm willing."

"So what is this, Mr. Wadsworth, about you being a lightning rod?" Dean Bell's voice lilted with skepticism.

"Honestly, I'm not sure," Kyle said. "But when I made the amulet, I, um...I..."

"Brought down a hailstorm from wanking," Alex finished for him.

"There wasn't any hail!"

"Okay, no hail. But there was thunder and lightning, and Michael here can attest the amulet works." Alex crossed his arms. "What odds would you give, Master Brandish, on a half-trained magic user stumbling through Bessarion's instructions on a hunch, and succeeding? One in ten thousand?"

Kyle didn't wait for her answer. "I get it. I had to, um, touch myself to conjure, too. So the theory is...I'll call down the power, and it goes from me to Jess so she can heal Frost? Does it have to be me?"

Master Brandish frowned. "It can be any lightning rod, so long as he's a virgin."

Kyle turned to Nichols. "Are you...?"

Nichols shook his head. "But I can't really be too jealous of you, can I? I mean...she's your girlfriend, you clearly arranged the entire Masque because you love her, and here I am stealing her from you. I can't really object to you having spell sex with Frost's life on the line."

Jess turned to Nichols and put her hands on his cheeks. "You can't be my first, but you'll be my last. There'll only ever be you after this, forever and ever." She pulled him into a kiss.

As Kyle looked away from the pair quickly. He thought he heard someone make a very quiet but disgusted sound, but when he looked he couldn't tell whether it had been Alex or Dean Bell. Bell caught his eye. "I take it you are willing, as well? I know Timothy Frost was not exactly a close friend."

Kyle looked at him lying there. "Yeah, but...I don't think my virginity is worth more than his life."

Brandish and Marjory Ransom were sharing a meaningful look. "Does the lightning rod really have to be a virgin?" Marjory asked.

"It could work with one who isn't, though the energy is purer if he is, and given how Frost got the way he is." Brandish brushed his hair back from his forehead. "But I see what you're saying. If Kyle gives up his virginity now, if he decides to go into the Esoteric Arts, some disciplines will be closed to him."

Marjory looked at Kyle. "If you really are a lightning rod, then Esoteric Studies is a good place for you."

"It sounds like I could still study Esoteric Arts, I just... wouldn't be able to do as much as some?" Kyle asked.

"Well, that's true," Marjory admitted. "There are complications, but..."

"I want to do it," Kyle said. "If Jess wants me, that is. I don't want it to seem like I'm doing it just for one last chance with her."

Jess shook her head. "It's you or nobody. I'm not doing it with some grad student from Nummus House just because he's a rod. Ew."

"How much time do we have to prepare?" Bell asked.

Ms. Finch got up and checked Frost over, though Kyle wasn't sure what all the things she did were. Checked his pulse, looked at his eyes, put her hand over his heart. "He's very weak. We could lose him at any time. He's in much worse shape than Alex was."

"That's because he didn't break my heart," Alex said, causing Michael to burst into tears again.

Kyle stood. "That's enough. What preparation do we need? If he really could die any time, I don't see any good in waiting."

Bell nodded. "I agree. I don't even think we should move to the Sassamon chamber. Callendra, you'll oversee. Ransom, you may need to assist Torralva and Wadsworth. Everyone else out, including Candlin. And myself." He stood and the others stood with him.

"Jess, I'll wait for you back at your room," Nichols said.

"You'll have the place to yourself," Alex added, his arm around Monica's shoulders.

"I'll pretend I didn't hear that," said Ms. Finch.

Kyle didn't have time to think about any of that as the others were ushered out, until only Bell and Candlin were left of those who were supposed to leave. Marjory began moving the furniture around. Kyle wanted to help, but he didn't know what was supposed to go where. He found himself suddenly hugging Jess instead, though over her shoulder he watched Michael.

"Quilian, I really think you ought to oversee..." Master Brandish was arguing to Bell.

"Nonsense. Someone has to keep watch on this one." He had his hand around Michael's upper arm.

"Shouldn't you wear the amulet?" Kyle called out.

Dean Bell shook his head. "I believe it will work only for you, or at the very least, more poorly for others."

"You're the ritualist," Brandish argued back. "I can handle the siren."

"I'm only part siren," Michael said miserably. "Isn't there anything I can do to help?"

Kyle felt sorry for him, not for the first time that night, as Brandish and Bell both turned the hardness of their glares on the poor thing.

"We only get one chance at this," Brandish insisted. "You need to oversee the preparations at the very least."

"Very well. Wadsworth, please reinforce the need for Candlin here not to interfere, though."

Kyle let go of Jess and put a hand on Michael's shoulder. "You need to be quiet and stay out of the way, okay? If you want to help Frost, that's the only way."

"Okay." Candlin's answer came back a whisper as he sank into a chair.

Master Brandish led Kyle a few steps away then. "You and Miss Torralva..."

Kyle threw up his hands. "Look, I know what's about to happen. I'm about to have sex with my very recently no-longer girlfriend right in front of everyone. Could we at least be on a first-name basis for now?"

Master Brandish's eyes widened, but he thought he heard a suppressed laugh come from Dean Bell's direction. The master cleared her throat. "Of course, Kyle, if you're more comfortable that way."

"Yes, yes, I am."

"Good. What I was about to say is about your comfort, partly. If the two of you wish to be alone for a while, there's a bedroom through the door here." She gestured to the far back of the room.

Kyle found his usual wait-and-see reaction to baffling information was not working just now. "Why is there a bedroom here?"

"Because Quilian is a workaholic who doesn't have the good sense to go home half the time," she said. "It's a bit utilitarian, but you'll have some privacy. Do what you like, just please don't penetrate her until you rejoin us out here, and please do make sure you're both quite aroused."

"Okay. Anything else I need to know?"

She thought for a moment. "There are three crucial moments in this ritual. One is the moment of penetration, one is when she comes, and one is when you come. Without getting too technical, though, you can actually make it five moments. The penetration counts for two, because you're both virgins, her first orgasm would be number three, and if you can come simultaneously with her when she comes a second time, that would be four and five. But I don't want to put too much pressure on your first time. The most important thing is that she comes first, because if you come first and she hasn't yet, and you go soft..."

Kyle took a deep breath, too absorbed in the details of the ritual magic to be embarrassed. "Got it. What if she comes before I even penetrate her?"

Master Brandish smiled. "Good thinking, but in this case, it doesn't get you anything magically and might actually disperse some of her energy. Make sure you're inside her when she comes. The rest you can leave to us."

"All right." Kyle took a step toward Jess.

"Oh, and Kyle," Master Brandish added. "If you're shy about what we see...I suggest you leave her dress on and put her on top."

He watched Jess blush a deep red at that.

Master Brandish was cutting some symbols into the carpet with the sword as he put his arm around Jess and led her into the small bedroom.

* * * *

The first thing Jess said once they were alone was, "I'm sorry."

"Shh, you already said that." Kyle kissed her hair. "I've spent six months trying to get you to figure out I'm the one, but if I'm not, then I'm not. It's really okay."

"Fate is a funny old thing," she said, quoting Alex. "He fell for me Halloween night. We've been friends since then, but until tonight I hadn't realized..." She broke off there, then said, "I'm just sorry for hurting you. I really do care a lot about you, you know."

"I know. But let's not think about me being hurt right now, all right?" He brushed stray hairs back from her cheek, tucking them behind her ear. "We're about to do a really beautiful thing. A really noble thing. I think we can count ourselves lucky to have the chance, don't you?"

She nodded, a smile spreading across her face. "And I really, really am glad that it's you. Oh, Kyle." She pulled him down into a kiss and he hugged her tightly against him.

He felt slightly amazed that the events of the evening hadn't diminished his desire for her at all. Even as his mind and his heart were preparing to let her go, his body responded the way he would have expected it to had she just accepted the proposal he never got to make. It felt like it took only seconds for him to get hard, pressing against her. To think he would finally be inside her—his cock twitched in his tights, throbbing with anticipation.

For one last time, she was his, and would be truly his. He lifted her up and lay her on the bed, her skirts spreading around her like a giant flower. "Jess..." The dress had laces and boning and crinolines and things, but under it all she was wearing the same panties she always wore. He slipped them from her legs and parted her lips gently, placing a kiss on her clit before snaking his tongue out to lick her.

Her cries resounded in the small room as he teased her, flicking his tongue lightly over the nub for a while and then soothing it with long, wet strokes. He lifted his head. "She told me not to let you come until after I'm in you, you know."

"Ahh! You tease! Get over here then and take some of your own medicine."

"No, no, no, I have to hold out until after you come, you know. I'm hard as a rock already, Jess. If you tease me, I might not last past slipping inside you." He did move to lie next to her, though, his hand toying with her laces. He kissed her. "That happens to some guys, doesn't it? Where it's so incredible that they just come right away? Or is that only in books?"

"No idea," she said, wriggling a little as the dress fell open. So much for the idea of leaving it on. Kyle didn't think it was a good idea to let Jess be on top anyway, since he truly was going to be challenged to last long enough. "But I do think you should do like you usually do. You've always lasted fine like that." She pulled open the front button on his breeches.

In short order, all their finery was on the floor and Kyle was atop her, rutting gently against her hip while looking into her eyes. "What position do you think we should use?"

"I think just like this." Her voice was breathy. "Only, you know."

"Inside."

"Yes."

"Think it'll be okay if I kiss your neck like this?"

"Yes."

"Mmm. And suckle your nipples like this?"

"Yes!"

Kyle slipped his cock between her legs, and found she was so slick that he was quickly coated. "Wait a second."

"What?"

"What about safe sex?"

"You really don't know anything about sex magic, do you?"

"Not a thing."

"Don't worry. The energy we're raising won't go into conception. And any STDs you have, I would have already gotten," she teased.

He chuckled. "All right. If you say so. I'm sure I can do this," he thrust a bit harder, teasing her back with his cock, "but I don't think I could have put a condom on with Dean Bell watching."

She wrapped her hands around his buttocks with a small grunt. "Maybe we ought to get out there."

He nodded and kissed her one more time.

They held hands as they rounded Dean Bell's desk to find the carpet in the sitting area had been transformed into a ritual circle, ringed with candles and symbols. Frost was still on the couch, Candlin in a chair on the other side of the circle from him, and Dean Bell standing between them. Meanwhile the two women were sitting crosslegged inside the circle and Marjory was fanning the smoke from an incense burner with a leaf of some kind. They were both still dressed but barefoot, and Marjory's skirt had been replaced by a pair of shorts.

Dean Bell stepped forward with a bowl in his hand. "So like Adam and Eve," he said, and Kyle had a feeling he was holding back a laugh. But he dipped his fingers in the bowl and painted something on Kyle's forehead, then on Jess's. He painted another symbol on Kyle's chest, then stepped back. "You may enter the circle."

Kyle kept hold of Jess's hand as they stepped over the line, and suddenly he could smell the incense.

"Just ignore us," Marjory said in a low voice.

Jess giggled at that. "Yeah, right." But she sat at the center of the circle, then lay back, holding her arms out toward Kyle.

She was as beautiful as ever, eyes shining in the candlelight, her skin perfect and her hair still bound up with some strings of pearls. With the incense filling his head, Kyle could almost imagine they were back in her room after the Masque, finally consummating their commitment to each other. He knelt between her legs and then stretched out on top of her, keeping his upper body propped up with one arm as he adjusted the angle of his cock between her legs.

He thrust a few times the old way, the hard length of him along her clit, then settled a bit lower.

"Go on," Jess said.

"Shhh." He kissed her and rocked his hips, shuddering as the head of his cock slid through silk wetness, not into her yet, but close. He kept rocking his hips slowly, feeling for the right spot, the right angle. He didn't want to reach down with his hand. He had his elbows under her arms and he nibbled at her neck. He didn't want to reach down, he wanted to—

She cried out as he plunged into her and he realized that other sound he heard was his own voice. He'd tried before to imagine something that felt better than rubbing off on her, and now he'd found it. He rocked his hips again, and pushed deeper, and she clung to him, the sound she was making not a bad sound at all.

He rocked his hips once more, partway out of her and back in, and realized he could see a kind of glowing ball above her head, floating there. It was like a ball of mist, with two different colors of smoke roiling around inside it. He couldn't quite say what the colors were, only that they were distinct.

But the glowing ball didn't hold his attention nearly so much as Jess under him. *Around* him. His hips seemed to be moving of their own accord, and he leaned over to nibble at her ear and whisper, "I'm in you."

"I know," she whispered back.

"Let's see if you can come now," he added, trying to slip his thumb between them to her clit, but she pulled his hand back, shaking her head.

"Just keep on like that," she said, wrapping her legs around his thighs and grinding upward against him. "Just. Like. That..."

"I can do that." He was very aroused, but not yet close, and the pace of her grinding was slower than the one he would have picked to make himself come. Her neck tasted of salt and flowers and he sucked at the tender place there that had always made her writhe before. She cried out and squeezed him harder, both with her arms and the muscles inside her, a new cry ringing out on every thrust, and a dozen or so thrusts later she went suddenly limp.

"Wow," she breathed. Kyle could see a third color had joined the two entwining in the ball.

"Good?" he asked with a grin.

"Don't fish for compliments," she warned, grinning back. "Think we can get it right? Come together?"

"I hope so," he said, picking up the pace a little.

Her eyes widened and she gripped him urgently. "I might...I might be closer to a second one than...than usual."

He slowed, kissing her softly. "You always go off pretty fast the second time."

"Kyle..."

"Be right there," he promised, and began to fuck her in earnest, his hips snapping as he bent one of her legs toward her chest. Yes, that was the angle his cock wanted, that feeling like he was getting as deep into her as he could, into the tightest, hottest place. And just when he thought it couldn't get any better, she tightened still more around him, her eyes pleading with him.

There was no denying the demand of her body, though, and he began to come quite suddenly, making an audible sound of surprise just a moment before she began to cry out again. Each thrust felt like it was just adding fuel to the explosion, and Kyle wouldn't have been surprised if he'd sprouted wings or the carpet had caught fire or any number of things.

What actually happened was two more streams of color flooded into the glowing ball, and Jess reached up and grasped it with both hands as if it were solid, then let it go. Kyle looked up as Dean Bell, now standing over Frost's inert form, waved a wand. The ball flew straight at Frost's chest and disappeared. Only a moment later, Frost clutched at his chest and sat bolt upright, eyes wild.

Michael jumped to his feet. "Tim!"

But Frost screamed and clutched onto Dean Bell, hiding his face in his robes. Brandish moved to block the siren from moving toward them.

Kyle kissed Jess, who had been watching it all upside down. "Hi," he said.

"Hi," she answered, almost shyly. But she pulled him down for another kiss and his soft cock slipped free. "Looks like we did it."

"Yeah." They kissed one last time, then set about disentangling their limbs and sitting up.

It wasn't until she stepped out of the circle that her absence hit him like a wave of cold water. Candlin had burst into tears again, and he suspected Frost was crying in Bell's arms, too. Was that why his own cheeks felt so wet?

Then someone was there with a blanket, wrapping it around his shoulders. Marjory. She held him and stroked his hair and said "I know," and even though he had no idea what it was she knew, it felt good to hear it.

When he looked up again, after losing track of time, he and Marjory were alone in the room, still sitting in the circle surrounded by candles that were no longer lit. His eyes burned from leftover incense and crying. "There wasn't time to warn you how...ripped apart you might feel," she said in a quiet voice. "I mean, even without all the stuff about her and the other guy..."

Kyle shook his head. "I knew. She told me." He could almost hear Jess saying, like she had that one time, *Sex makes you vulnerable, you know. It opens your heart, in all ways.*

And Kyle had answered with a lie. *I don't want to cry over someone I don't care about anymore,* he'd said. But if he didn't care, he wouldn't have been crying. And the same was true now.

"The rest of them are raiding the kitchen at Gladius House," Marjory said, then, reaching for her glasses and putting them back on. "Do you want to join them?"

He sat back and looked around at the ruined carpet and sighed. "Honestly, I think I'd rather just get a pizza and sleep for a week."

She smiled at him. "Can you make it to Camella House? Or should I get it delivered here?"

He smiled back. Someone had piled all his party clothes near them, as well as a bathrobe. He pulled on the robe. "Camella House isn't far. Let's go."

April

"WHAT I don't understand is how he makes it taste the way you think flowers should taste, except that they don't." Kyle stared at the vial in his hand as the wind blew his hair into his eyes. He hadn't had it cut all year, not since last September right before he'd arrived at Harvard. At Veritas.

"What's to understand? That's magic," Alex answered, getting up from the camp chair he'd been sitting in and walking to the edge of the roof to look down. "I'm telling you, Randall is going to be one of the most gifted alchemists of our generation."

"I believe that," Kyle said, taking the last sip from the vial and looking around for the flowers he was sure must be strewn all around him. Whatever the stuff was—Randall hadn't named it yet—it was also very relaxing. Tonight was a good night to relax. Midterms were over, finals were still more than a month away, and tonight the wind was actually warm enough that they could laze around on the roof without needing Red Heat.

Alex held up his empty vial, then snapped his fingers to make it vanish.

Kyle threw his at him. "That's unfair. Even if it's just sleight of hand, it's still unfair."

Alex grinned. "You need to learn some sleight of hand. It's useful."

"Yeah, well." Kyle was learning there were surprising ways the magical world stayed hidden. One of the most pervasive was in getting exposed as frauds. Which made perfect sense, once Kyle thought about it, but he wouldn't have come up with it himself.

"So, you have a date for May Day yet?" Alex asked.

Kyle shrugged. "I'm sure Marjory would say yes if I asked." He'd woken up in her bed the night after the Masque, with fragmentary memories of getting each other off during the night. But she didn't push, and neither did he.

He'd needed some time to himself after that. The story was all over the school, of course, about how he'd caught Candlin and exposed him as the siren, but so was the story about Jess and Nichols. Kyle found his popularity had never been higher, and at the same time his interest in finding a relationship had never been lower.

At least exactly how Frost had been restored was still a secret.

"Then again, she's probably got someone lined up already," Kyle added. "I suppose you and Monica are all set?"

"Yeah, should be. Unless she's pissed at me that week. I guess I'll tread carefully." Alex came and sat down again, took a vial out of the box between their chairs, and thumbed the cork out. "Mm. This one smells like gardenia."

"I don't even know what a gardenia is," Kyle said.

"The Alchemy department does have botany classes, too, you know."

"Yeah." Kyle took another vial for himself. "Hmm. Roses. That one I know. I guess I don't have much time to figure out what I'm taking next semester."

"What do you have in mind?"

Kyle sipped from the vial. Rose petals, everywhere. Except they weren't. "More poetry. I'm going to continue with the prophecy commentary stuff, too. But...I've been thinking about going into a seminar in Esoteric Studies."

Alex grinned. "That should be fun."

"For a while, anyway." Kyle looked across the campus rooftops, listening to the wind blowing through the newly sprouted leaves on the trees. "Seems like everyone I know who actually specializes in Esoteric Arts is lonely, though."

"Lonely, or just single?" Alex asked, looking at him more seriously.

"Hmm. Brandish is lonely. I'm sure of it. What happened between her and Bell, anyway?"

Alex downed the rest of his vial and then tossed it from the roof into the dark. "I don't know exactly, but when they were involved, she was male. I think maybe she started out biologically female, then went male for a while, but then went back? There are rumors galore of course, but near as I can tell, it had something to do with that."

"And not with the fact that he's a sanctimonious prick?"

Alex snorted, then coughed. "Oh, just maybe."

Kyle had gone to Bell's office the day after the Masque, after getting cleaned up and eating some more. The carpet had still been a wreck but otherwise there was no evidence of what had gone on the night before. He wasn't sure why he'd felt the need to do what he did, but he went to speak on Candlin's behalf, and Alex's, and to just basically make sure that neither of them was getting expelled or the Geas or any of that. He'd gone there to offer to speak to all the Judges, if necessary, but Bell had been the only one he'd talked to.

It hadn't been an easy conversation. But in the end Candlin was put on academic leave and sent to work with some Esoteric Arts specialists who could help him rein in his sirenic side. Frost was on leave, too, as he was going to need another month to recover at least, and ended up withdrawing for the semester. Alex was taking a light course load and had been given until next fall to work on his junior project.

To this day, Kyle wasn't completely sure what had convinced Bell to go along with his demands. Only that he'd said all the right things.

He tossed his vial over the edge. "Maybe for May Day I'll just come up here by myself and wank until it rains..."

"You wouldn't!" Alex looked horrified for a moment, then laughed when he saw Kyle was pulling his leg. "Besides, I'm sure anyone with weather aptitude is going to be trying to make it warm, sunny, and free of mosquitoes."

Kyle was pretty sure the bit about the mosquitoes was a joke. They sat in companionable silence for a while, watching the cheese wheel of the moon emerge from behind the steeple of Memorial Church.

Alex stood. "Believe it or not, I think I'm going to go write a paper."

Kyle got to his feet, too. "Maybe I'll write a poem."

They folded their chairs and were just headed to the stairs when Alex stopped dead and Kyle walked into him. "What?"

Alex pointed.

Michael Candlin was standing there in front of the stairwell door, in black robes that covered his hands and feet. "Kyle Wadsworth," he said.

"Michael? Are you all right?"

He spoke as if he hadn't heard what Kyle had said. "I wanted to say thank you. I know it was you who got Bell to go easy on me. Things are...much better now. They're letting me register for next semester."

"That's good," Kyle said. "Good."

"But I wanted to thank you by doing something for you. There isn't much I can do, really, but sirens are Seers, too, you know. So this prophecy is for you."

"Michael, you really don't have to..."

But his eyes had fallen closed and he swayed. Kyle stepped forward to steady him but Alex held him back.

They waited.

When Candlin's eyes re-opened, they were unseeing. He spoke, as if reciting:

And the one will have the power of the word
and the other the power of the touch
But though one speak and the other move
Until they meet neither will know their true strength
There is one moon and one sun, and the sky holds both
In the palm of God's hand, one diamond, one pearl
Though one eclipse the other, each shines with inner beauty
The sky is not whole without both
The lovers run as the open sky boils with thunder
In the cities they dash between buildings and in
the country flee the pastures for the safety of the woods
Into the darkness they must go to escape the scouring

Take shelter in the trees, run the narrow channel,
A storm is coming.

Kyle's blood had run cold at first. The words weren't exactly the same as what he knew, but they were close enough to the Avestan First Cycle. Then he stared in plain shock as Candlin disappeared.

"What happened?"

Alex let out a breath. "He wasn't really here, I think. He had all the sirenic powers, after all, including mind reading, projecting visions..."

"So he was just in our heads? But you saw him, too."

Alex nodded. "So you recognized what he was saying?"

Kyle pulled open the door to the stairs. "Yeah, except for that bit at the end. That was new."

"It's not...normal, for one oracle to quote from another." Alex followed him into the stairwell. "You know that, right? If that was a real prophecy, though, it could mean that the events prophesied in the original one might be coming to pass finally. Which prophecy was that from?"

Kyle stopped and looked back up at him. "You mean you don't know?"

"What, is it the Avestan Cycle or something?"

"Yes, you nut! It's only the most famous prophecy in magical history." Kyle laughed.

"What's so funny?" Alex held out his hands.

"Just, I finally knew something you didn't! It's a banner day!" Kyle jumped down the last few steps to the landing, gleeful.

"Okay, okay! I never got around to reading it. Big deal, I know the gist..."

Kyle was still laughing when they got downstairs and parted ways. He walked back to Gladius House feeling mellow and content. He was glad Michael was doing okay, and Randall's concoctions were still soothing him from the inside. He sat by his open window, writing down what Michael's apparition had said, but not feeling particularly worried by it. Prophecies always had multiple interpretations, after all.

He looked up at the sudden spatter of raindrops on the window. New England weather, as everyone kept telling him over and over, was more unpredictable and full of sudden changes than anywhere in the world. *Maybe that's what Michael meant when he said "A storm is coming"—Get off the roof, you dummies?*

Kyle laughed. A literal interpretation! How novel! He would have to tell Master Lester about it in class tomorrow. For now, he just shut the window and lay back on his bed, lulled to sleep by the sound of the rain on the roof.

THE END

TO BE CONTINUED...
in Magic University: Book Two

Afterword

EVERY ROMANCE is a "labor of love" of sorts, but it's no secret here that in Magic University I am riffing on some of the books I have loved most, particularly J. K. Rowling's *Harry Potter* series. Potter fans will have noticed many references, and sharp-eyed readers will find bits of homage buried in here to many of my other favorite fantasy writers, like Steven Brust, Roger Zelazny, Anne Bishop, Anne McCaffrey, Marion Zimmer Bradley, and Jacqueline Carey, to name just a few. These writers are the poets of my soul.

My goal here was to write something that would satisfy all the cravings, though, that the *Harry Potter* books brought out in me. Although I love them dearly, the books do have certain deficiencies. By necessity, books written for a young audience will be lacking in sex, for example. Grown-up readers wanted more exploration of questions of good and evil. I would have loved to have known there were gay characters in the Potterverse without having to either read between the lines to figure it out, or to read the author's interviews post-publication.

Fortunately for me, J. K. Rowling didn't invent magic or spells or wands, or even the concept of a magical school (check out *Wizard's Hall* by Jane Yolen for one notable example that predates Harry by several years). So this is my magical world for grown-ups, where the magic doesn't come quite as easily as it does in the Potterverse. Harry Potter is hardly the first protagonist whose mastery of magic was a metaphor for his coming of age (think *A Wizard of Earthsea* by Ursula K. LeGuin), nor is he the first main character to suddenly discover his magical heritage or connection to the magical world after growing up an orphan--Cinderella comes to mind, among other fairy tale protagonists, and so does Frodo Baggins, along with many modern incarnations of the orphan hero or heroine in modern fantasy. (Even Shakespeare used the archetype in *A Winter's Tale*, in which the princess Perdita is raised by shepherds after her mother--named Hermione--is imprisoned by the king.) Indeed, one of the reasons the *Harry Potter* books resonate so strongly is that they utilize many of the archetypes and ideas embodied in the ancient stories and recent fantasy antecedents, and I've done the same.

The *Potter* books also sometimes make up their magic from whole cloth, and sometimes draw on real "magical" history. For example, Nicholas Flamel, who Rowling uses as a background character, was an actual historical figure purported to have been the alchemist who created the Philosopher's Stone. I do the same, sometimes inventing and sometimes supposing that before magical scholarship and mundane scholarship were separated, mundane historians knew just as much about famous wizards and witches as they did about kings and politicians. (Check my blog at www.ravenousromance.com for some fascinating info on what I dug up about Jess's ancestor, Harvard history, Tarot symbolism, and more. Harvard really does divide its students into different Houses!)

There, I think, the resemblance ends. If Rowling's work ultimately was about the redemptive power of a mother's love for her children (Harry's mother saves him as an infant, Draco's mother's concern over her son causes her to aid Harry's cause, etc...), mine here is about the power of romantic love and the magic of love and sex entwined. My characters are entirely my own (thank goodness Kyle doesn't have the anger management problems or the jealousy that Harry does), and my overarching plot is less about Good versus Evil than about... well, actually, I can't tell you that without potentially ruining the surprises yet to come. So I'll stay mum. I do hope you had a wonderful time visiting my hidden magical garden here, and that you'll come visit again for books two, three, and four! Kyle still has a lot to learn about magic, and about love, and I hope you'll enjoy each step on his journey.

Cecilia Tan
Cambridge, Mass.

Also Available from Red Silk Editions

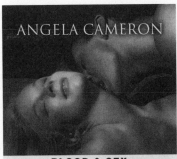

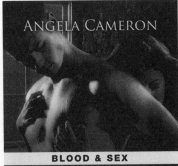

Blood & Sex: Michael
by Angela Cameron

This is a spine-chilling and erotic tale of a Mafia vampire and the detective who is determined to bring to justice a serial killer. Detective Victoria Tyler allows Mafia vampire Michael to "take her neck" and lead her on a journey through a world of bondage, domination, and blood to stop the killer. But can she resist the dark lusts he sparks?

Volume 1 in the Blood & Sex series

Paperback: $12.95

978-1-59003-203-9

Available in August 2010

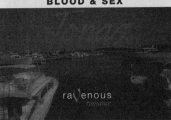

Blood & Sex: Jonas
by Angela Cameron

Jonas, the strangely appealing owner of the new vampire-themed bondage club could be the perfect distraction for workaholic Dr. Elena Jensen. But their worlds couldn't be farther apart....

Volume 2 of the Blood & Sex series

Paperback: $12.95

978-1-59003-202-2

Available in October 2010

Blood & Sex: Blane
by Angela Cameron

Will Blane be able to break through the guarded reserve of Christiana, the beautiful woman the vampire leader has sent to educate the newest vampires? Or will her sense of duty be stronger than the passion that threatens to sweep her away?

Volume 3 of the Blood & Sex series

Paperback: $12.95

978-1-59003-206-0

Available in December 2010

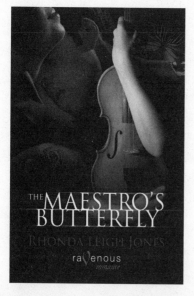

The Maestro's Butterfly
by Rhonda Leigh Jones

Miranda O'Connell has just made a dangerous bet with her mysterious, sexy music teacher that will change her life forever. Will she fall in love with the kinky vampire Maestro and submit to life as a feeder slave? Or will she escape the confines of his estate for the dashing, dangerous charms of his brother?

Paperback: $12.95

978-1-59003-207-7

Available in November 2010

The Maestro's Maker
by Rhonda Leigh Jones

Trapped between two vampires: Chloe discovers the darkness that binds the beautiful and arrogant French noble Claudio du Fresne and his oldest friend Francois Villaforte. With danger, intrigue, and kinky sex, *The Maestro's Maker* takes vampire erotica to passionate new levels!

Paperback: $12.95

978-1-59003-210-7

Available in December 2010

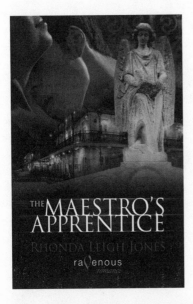

The Maestro's Apprentice
by Rhonda Leigh Jones

For the first time in her life, Autumn is free. She has escaped Claudio du Fresne, the vampire for whom she had been a feeder-slave for years. Now she wants to play, and for her, playing means wild, crazy sex with strangers.

Paperback: $12.95

978-1-59003-209-1

Available in January 2011

The Dark Desires of the Druids: Sex & Subterfuge
by Isabel Roman

"Do you like jealous heroes and love triangles? How about sizzling sexual encounters atop dining room furniture? If you answered yes to either question, you're going to love this novella." —Susan S., loveromance.passion.com

Paperback: $12.95

978-1-59003-200-8

Available in August 2010

The Dark Desires of the Druids: Desert and Destiny
by Isabel Roman

The first time they met, Arbelle Bahari tried to kill him. The second time, they made love on a desk in the British Museum.

"The action is fast and exciting, the mystery is engaging, and the romance is searingly hot." —Whipped Cream Reviews (5 Cherries)

Paperback: $12.95

978-1-59003-201-5

Available in October 2010

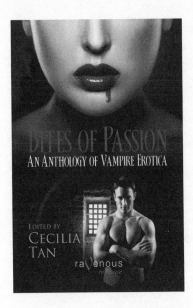

Bites of Passion
edited by Cecilia Tan

What does it mean to love a vampire? Does it mean nights of pleasure tempered with sweet pain? Eight top authors explore the themes of immortal love, the lust for blood, and the eternal struggle between light and dark.

Paperback: $12.95

978-1-59003-205-3

Available in September 2010

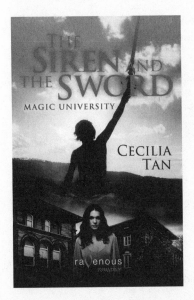

Magic University: The Siren and the Sword
by Cecilia Tan

Harvard freshman Kyle Wadsorth is eager to start a new life. Surprises abound when he discovers a secret magical university hidden inside Harvard and he meets Jess Torralva, who tutors him in the ways of magic, sex, and love.

Paperback: $12.95

978-1-59003-208-4

Available in November 2010

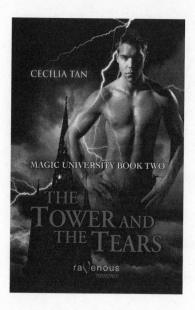

Magic University: The Tower and the Tears by Cecilia Tan

This second volume in the Magic University series brings together myth, magic, and eroticism for adult readers of fantasy who want a bedtime tale of their own.

"Simply one of the most important writers, editors, and innovators in contemporary American erotic literature."—Susie Bright

Paperback: $12.95

978-1-59003-211-4

Available in January 2011

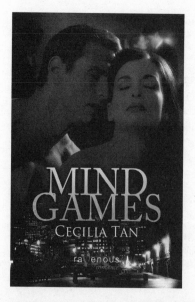

Mind Games by Cecilia Tan

Who hasn't fantasized about using psychic abilities to satisfy your every sexual desire? *Mind Games* provides readers the opportunity to live out that dream....

"Scorching hot with a touch of suspense. Cecilia Tan brings together love, suspense, and scorching sex in a story well worth reading."—*ParaNormal Romance Review*

Paperback: $12.95

978-1-59003-204-6

Available in September 2010

Notes

Notes